Praise f

The old adage, "Be careful what you wish for," takes on new life in *Lucky Stiff*. Barbara Bellesi Zito shows us the perilous and hilarious track we find ourselves on when the thing we (think) we want most, finds its way to us. Laugh-out-loud funny!

—Ashleigh Renard, author of *Swing*

In *Lucky Stiff*, Barbara Bellesi Zito tells the story of Larry Sortino, a CPA in possession of an enviable windfall—except "lucky" Larry wants no part of it. Larry endures entertaining twists and turns as he navigates his big break and attempts to discover if he's lucky, or not. With a sharp wit and deft voice, the author offers clever commentary on work life, marriage, and our fixation with wealth. *Lucky Stiff* is a sure-footed debut novel not to be missed.

—Charlotte Rains Dixon, MFA, author of
The Bonne Chance Bakery, writing teacher, and coach

Lucky Stiff is a tragically comic romance that points out the absurdity of not knowing your own worth. Larry is a magnificent and unforgettable character who is both entirely unique and startlingly familiar. I couldn't stop reading, and as I finished the last page, I couldn't stop smiling. A joy of a novel!

—Rachel Eve Moulton, author of *Tinfoil Butterfly*

What do you do when you win the lottery? Larry Sortino finds out in Barbara Bellesi Zito's delightful and tension-filled romp through a winner's decision-making process. With charming good humor, the story twists and turns, and leaves the reader guessing until the last moment. Well-drawn and likable characters populate the book. *Lucky Stiff* is an escape into what-if, and a thought-provoking read that reminds us that having wealth can be fun, but it brings angst and responsibilities as well.

—Patricia Barletta, award-winning author of
the Auriano Curse series

Barbara Bellesi Zito's *Lucky Stiff* takes us through the ups and downs of one man's struggle to grapple with his new fate. The story made me reflect on my own choices and what I would do given the chance to change it all. Zito captivates us through her descriptive prose while keeping us laughing along the way. If you want to be thoroughly entertained, this is the novel for you!

—Blayr Austin, comedy writer and teacher at The Second city

LUCKY STIFF

Barbara Bellesi Zito

Literary Wanderlust | Denver, Colorado

Published in the United States by Literary Wanderlust LLC, Denver, Colorado. www.LiteraryWanderlust.com

ISBN print: 978-1-956615-14-2
ISBN digital: 978-1-956615-17-3

Cover design: Craig Terlson

Printed in the United States of America

Dedication

For Dad

Part 1

January

Chapter 1

L arry Sortino stared down upon his kingdom.
      "One day, I will own you," he said.

The kingdom in question was the one-bedroom condo on Staten Island he shared with his wife, Sarah. Actually, he had been examining a blurry printout of the condo's floor plan, which had sections colored in with neon green highlighter. Once a month, after he paid the mortgage, he would unfold the sheet of paper he kept in a desk drawer and visualize what percentage of the place they owned.

Sarah was content to make the minimum mortgage payment each month. He had run the numbers, showed her how they could avoid thousands of dollars in interest if they paid just a little bit more each time. He tried to woo her into refinancing their mortgage for a shorter term, even had a home appraisal done last spring. She did a little dance when she found out how much the value had gone up, but that was it.

He'd thought that she'd find his accounting prowess sexy, perhaps.

She hadn't.

"This is the American Dream," she said. "This is what we signed up for." She kicked in half of the mortgage every month and, if she had a little extra cash, she would buy something new for the place. She had been on a throw pillow kick of late, and it was no longer possible to sit down on the couch.

He calculated that they had 27 percent equity in their home. He even wrote the figure on a sticky note and waved it in front of her. "Don't you care that the mortgage lender has 73 percent of our American Dream?"

The look she gave him made it clear that she did not.

But he was an overachiever on a mission. There was no way he was going to take the full thirty years to pay off their place. He kept the sticky note on his desk.

One night last summer, long after Sarah had gone to bed, he sat at his desk in the corner of the living room to finish up some work for one of his clients. This particular client was a successful business owner who had just paid off the mortgage on his primary residence and was preparing to buy a vacation home. He envied the guy. He wondered what it would feel like to live under a roof that was paid for in full and to have enough money to buy another.

Larry didn't care to become a real estate mogul. He just wanted to be king of his own castle, or rather, condo. It would feel so good not to have a mortgage. He didn't want to be rich, but he loved the idea of being able to hold on to more of his paycheck and not to wait until he was in his sixties to do it. Never mind that he had no idea how he would spend the extra money. Would he drive a nicer car? Would they go on big vacations? Wear clothing bought at full price? He had no clue. What he did know was that he liked options, and money would give him plenty.

27 percent. He stared at the sticky note, and he chewed his lip. He tapped his pen. Tap tap tap. His tapping habit annoyed Sarah, but she was asleep, so he was safe from her exasperated

sighs. He enjoyed these quiet late nights, even if it meant he was still poring over spreadsheets. The night was his and his alone.

A foghorn blasted from the Staten Island Ferry leaving the dock in St. George. Nope, the night was not his alone after all.

27 percent. He sighed. He ripped off the sticky note and shoved it far back in the desk drawer. His hand brushed against an envelope marked with the return address of the condo association. He took it out and opened it. Inside was the welcome letter they'd received when they moved into the building, along with a copy of their condo's floor plan.

He stared at the computer-generated sketch, traced the straight lines and angles separating the rooms with the tip of his index finger. Then he had an idea. He grabbed a green highlighter from his work bag and uncapped it. With the narrow neon tip, he outlined one-fourth of the floor plan, plus a little extra. Or 27 percent, to be exact. The highlighter squeaked as he filled in the area with short, smooth strokes, careful to stay within the lines. The act was relaxing, even meditative.

He surveyed his work. In his estimation, they had already paid off the entire terrace, bedroom with the en suite bath, and a few precious ceramic tiled steps into the kitchen. Not bad. But he needed to do better.

Since that summer night, the idea of how quickly he could color in more of the floor plan had consumed him. Whenever he brewed coffee in the corner of the kitchen, he stood on tiles they owned. When he put his coffee mug in the sink, he had to cross over into mortgaged territory.

It both maddened and motivated him.

Still, when he took out that piece of paper each month to color in another sliver of the floor plan, he beamed. He and Sarah owned a little piece of the world for themselves. Maybe they would own a bigger piece one day—ugh, though that would mean a bigger mortgage to go with it. Well, they would need to move to a bigger place or even a house, if and when Sarah ever got pregnant. Their one-bedroom condo was perfect for a youngish married couple, but it would shrink with the arrival of a little one. He sighed. Despite all the poking and prodding Sarah had submitted herself to over the past year and a half, Baby Sortino was still a wistful dream. And, for now, their condo would remain spacious and tidy.

He folded up the floor plan, tapped it three times on the surface of the desk, then tucked it away under a stack of his firm's marketing brochures. He closed the drawer and got up. He yawned and stretched as he took in the rest of their home.

"I will own you," he told the living room.

He glared at the kitchen and dining room. "I will *own* you."

Yes, he had developed a habit of talking to the various rooms and walls of their condo. Once, Sarah had walked by during one of these soliloquies. She'd rolled her eyes like she did every time she caught him talking to himself.

Fine. He didn't care. She could mock him all she wanted. On those nights when he sat and looked at their home and saw the progress they had made toward owning every last square inch of it, he slept like a baby, his dreams tinged with neon green.

—

It was a new year. That first Monday morning began like every other Monday morning. Larry poured himself a mug of dark roast coffee with half a glug of milk. He walked with purpose from the kitchen through the dining room and living room, unlocked the French doors to the terrace, and stepped outside. He took in a deep breath and let it out with a yawn. He shivered. It had been a brutal winter so far.

He sat down on one of the frigid wrought iron chairs, careful to arrange his thick fleece robe around his flannel pajamas for a double layer of protection from the frosty air blowing in from the harbor.

"Good morning, New York," he said. The city that never sleeps looked tired. He much preferred the illuminated nighttime skyline, even if seeing it meant he was at home, far away from the action.

He shivered again, then gulped down half the mug of steaming caffeine. Ahh. Better.

Was he foolish for drinking his morning coffee *al fresco* in January? Of course he was. But he and Sarah had paid thirty thousand dollars more to buy one of the condos with a terrace. He would use that terrace every day, damn it. Even if it meant the risk of hypothermia.

It wasn't so much the extra money that bothered him, which was saying a lot. After all, he was an accountant. Practical budgeting was his thing. But he was the one who had pushed for a terrace when they were condo hunting, not Sarah, the interior designer for whom such things would seem to matter more. They both wanted a short commute to Manhattan, but he also wanted fresh air—a near impossibility with apartment life in New York City. A condo on the North Shore of Staten Island with a terrace was a good compromise.

What did bother him was that the other terrace people never seemed to use theirs. These neighbors had paid thousands and thousands of dollars for an upgrade they used on rare occasions, if at all. A wasted luxury. Unless, of course, they had already paid off their mortgages and didn't need to worry about what they got for their money. That was their prerogative, he supposed. He snorted at their indifference.

He had started his morning ritual of coffee on the terrace the day after they moved in. It was summer at the time, so the weather hadn't posed a problem. Back then, Sarah would join him most mornings with a matching mug, though to hers, she would add an avalanche of sugar. That first season in the condo, they would stare out at the neighboring buildings of the development, willing their neighbors to come out and enjoy the outside fifty square feet of their homes, too. Few ever did, and they were never the ones who owned the top-floor penthouses, whose terraces stretched along two sides of the building, enough room for a well-attended cocktail party.

He took another sip. The coffee was already lukewarm. He went back into the condo for a refill. As he passed through the living room, he poked the power button on the remote for the flat-screen television anchored to the wall. The public television channel came on, and an announcer with white hair and wire-rimmed glasses urged Larry to donate. He wasn't much into public television, but the night before, he'd been flipping through the channels and happened to catch the end of a riveting round table discussion on proposed tax breaks for cultural foundations in New York State.

Refill in hand, he stood in front of the television. The pledge break ended, and the channel switched back to a documentary. It was about a folk singer he had never heard of, though judging by the size of the crowds cheering for her in the many concert clips that flashed across the screen, he felt a bit silly that he didn't know who she was.

He hadn't watched many documentaries, but he was intrigued by them as a film genre. The few he had watched made him feel like an intellectual. He aspired to be the type of person who would buy tickets in advance to a special screening of some hot new documentary at the Tribeca Film Festival while the rest of the world waited in long lines for the latest comic book hero movie. The idea of spending two or so hours immersed in a topic that brought some filmmaker and a dogged camera crew to the far reaches of the world—or in this case, Des Moines—was exciting.

At one time, Larry aspired to being more than an armchair traveler. He had even studied abroad in Rome the summer after his junior year. He went there to take a class in European economics, though he spent most of his time wandering the piazzas with a gelato in his hand, taking it all in. But as the years passed, watching shows about world travel as he relaxed on their sectional sofa had far more allure than getting on an actual plane and going somewhere. Last week he found their passports in the back of the junk drawer in the kitchen. They had expired three years ago.

Now the filmmaker was interviewing the singer's sister, who sang backup in the band. Next, he interviewed her manager, then her college roommate, then someone who once sold her some guitar picks. Every one of the talking heads was either riding in an elevator or sitting in the back of a moving car. Where the heck was everyone going? Couldn't they stay still for a minute?

The toilet flushed on the other side of the wall. He looked, half hoping Sarah would pop her head out the door of their bedroom to say good morning. She didn't. He knew she would instead dive back under the covers for at least another two hours. He had tried, without success, to convince her that the most successful people were early risers.

"One of the perks of being your own boss, hon," she would say. It didn't matter much in the end. None of her rich clients wanted to discuss wallpaper or upholstery swatches before noon, anyway.

There was a time not too long ago when she used to call him *hon*. When she started to call him Larry again, plain old Larry, or the lazier Lah, he sensed their union had taken a turn. They had once been the kind of couple who always used pet names for each other, resorting to their given names only in moments of frustration or when they needed to get each other's attention in a public place without embarrassing each other. Not that it ever embarrassed him to be called *hon* by his beautiful blonde wife in the middle of the grocery store. But as their relationship started to show some wear and tear at the seams, the saccharine nicknames had floated away until they were plain old Larry and Sarah once more, living their plain old lives together.

He knew it was possible for people to grow apart, had seen it happen with too many of his friends. Of all the statistics that made headlines, this was one he believed—about half of marriages ended in divorce. The numbers were assuring in their correctness, even if they weren't in his favor. Marriage was a risk, but he was happy to take it. Although in his line of work, he should have seen what was coming.

He reached for the handle on the door but changed his mind. He'd had enough of the cold terrace for today. He made a mental note to get cushions for the chairs so that he could tolerate sitting out there for longer. He would ask Sarah to help him choose the fabric. Maybe then she would come and sit with him again, like they used to. It had been too long since they sat out there together. For all he knew, she didn't even drink coffee anymore. He calculated that his marriage had started to sputter out sometime in September, though they hadn't gotten around to talking about it. Which was fine with him because he had no idea what to say.

He walked to the entrance of their bedroom. She was sprawled out on her stomach on her side of the bed, hair splayed out against the pillow. It would be so easy to crawl back into bed with her. Not to make love, but to lie next to her, an arm or leg intertwined with one of hers. Like they used to do.

He took a step toward the bed. Yes, he would do this.

Then, his phone dinged from the kitchen counter. Work emails already. His clients were the type who got up early, or else they didn't sleep much to begin with. Jumpstarting his marriage would have to wait.

It was tax season, after all.

Chapter 2

Larry sat in a chair in the conference room across from Rick, his manager. A cup of coffee grew cold in front of him. His mouth was dry, so he forced down a sip and stifled a shudder. Funny how he would think nothing of buying a cup of iced coffee to change things up, but when coffee grew cold on its own, it was repulsive.

He ground his teeth, an old habit he thought he had tossed out long ago along with his CPA exam prep books, but here it was again.

"You're joking, right?" Larry would try humor first. He was always a good sport.

A good sport who just got laid off.

"It's a merger, Larry. It's happening at Hanson and Co., too. We tried."

"You said it was fine to take off Christmas week."

"And it was. It's got nothing to do with that. It's a layoff, not a termination."

"HR told me I would lose the days if I didn't take them."

"No one said you did anything wrong." Rick's voice had taken on that gentle tone that people use around children.

Larry's right knee started to bounce. He gripped his thigh with a sweaty palm.

"You're not the only one." Rick looked uncomfortable.

"Mm hmm."

"Greg, Peter, Linda, a bunch more. About 25 percent of the floor. Effective immediately."

27 percent.

Larry's right hand began to twitch on his bouncing leg.

Bounce, twitch, bounce, twitch.

"But it's the beginning of tax season." Larry hated to state the obvious, but there it was. Of course, a firm like Parker & Rosenthal was busy all year round. Corporate clients kept them on their toes every quarter. But now it was crunch time. He had been looking forward to longer hours. More work would take his mind off Sarah and the fragile state of their union.

He shivered. Maybe the icy wrought iron chair had seeped into his bones. He focused on a framed poster on the wall behind Rick. A drawing of a tree for each of the four seasons. Lush cherry blossoms for spring, one laden with fruit for summer, a fiery orange one for the fall, and a barren snow-covered one for winter. But there was a fifth tree, with branches sprouting dollar signs. Tax season, of course. They'd all had a good chuckle when Rick hung it up on the wall five years ago. Stupid accounting humor.

"I fought for you and the others," Rick said. "Management called this."

Larry snapped out of his daydream.

"You *are* management."

"The *other* management called it."

Larry laughed. It was a real guffaw, not a biting, sarcastic chuckle. It was funny. It was all too funny.

"How many weeks are you giving me?"

"Eight."

"Twelve."

"I can't—"

"You can do twelve, Rick. I've been here for fifteen years. I was an intern, for God's sake."

"Okay, twelve."

"Thank you." Larry was surprised. That was easy. Should he have asked for more? He ground his teeth harder. The problem with having one employer for his entire career was that he didn't know how to negotiate. He'd never had to. The promotions seemed to come whenever he started to feel antsy in his current role, and so his moves up the ladder were without much drama.

Until now.

Rick stood with his hand out. "Larry, I never dreamt it would end like this."

There was so much he wanted to say to Rick right now. But none of it was appropriate for the workplace. His head was on the verge of exploding. What part of his brain was it that was overstimulated right now? He would have to find a documentary about neuroscience. God knows he would have the time to watch it now.

But he held it together. What would be the point of losing it now?

He reached out, shook Rick's hand, and left.

Larry Sortino. Always the good sport.

He walked back to his cubicle, taking a shortcut through the copy machine room to avoid running into his coworkers. He was not eager to make his exit in front of so many sympathetic onlookers, though by the way Rick made it seem, there weren't too many people left in the office anyway. He remembered a movie, one of those cheesy made-for-television productions he watched with his mom when he was a kid and allowed to stay up late on weekends. In this one movie, a woman who'd just been fired from her job wept as she walked down a long aisle of cubicles to the office exit. She carried a brown ledger box full of her personal belongings, a wilted potted plant sticking out of it.

Sad music played while coworkers averted their gazes.

He made it back to his cubicle. He looked over the divider at one of the assistants, a slender, pale woman who had been with the company much longer than he had. She did indeed have a ledger box and was stuffing it with items from her desk. But the box was white, not brown. He was a bit disappointed.

The woman glared at him, then shook her head. He nodded back. There was no potted plant in her box—not enough natural light in the office for any real flora to thrive.

The good news was that he didn't need a ledger box, white, brown, or any other color. He had learned not to load up his desk with too much stuff over the years. In his first five years at the firm alone, he had switched cubicles ten times. When he was on the audit team, he had clients all over town and had learned to travel light. Now in the digital age, most people opted to work from home two or three days per week. When they did come to the office, they signed out random cubicles on a first-come, first-serve basis. On an ordinary workday, the place was a ghost town. Now, with this series of layoffs, he half expected to see tumbleweeds of pink slips roll on by.

He walked to his cubicle du jour and powered down his laptop. He had received an apologetic email from HR asking him to leave all tech devices issued by the company on the desk with their respective chargers and cases. He took the power cord out of his bag and put it next to the computer.

His back pocket buzzed. A pause. Then a series of buzzes. He figured he had the dubious honor of being on someone's farewell text message chain. He didn't bother looking. Whether it was someone griping against management (probably Greg), someone already working their connections and making vague promises of hooking them all up with a recruiter (possibly Linda), or someone making plans to get together and commiserate over cocktails (definitely Peter), he wanted none of it.

The last thing left on his desk was a Parker & Rosenthal mug full of pens and pencils. He rifled through it. He took two of the better pens, the ones with the gel ink that didn't skip when he scribbled in the margins of a spreadsheet, and shoved them into a pocket in his bag. He spotted a fresh neon green highlighter. *27 percent.* The figure flashed in his head, then faded. He bit his lip and pocketed the highlighter as well.

Now he needed to get out of there.

He made his way to the elevator for the last time and jabbed the down button. On a normal day, there would be a throng of people chatting nearby this time of the morning, but not today. Those who were around seemed to be doing their best to avoid looking in his direction. He appreciated the sentiment.

The doors slid open and out walked a coworker. She froze when she saw him. Damn it, what was her name? Was it Allison from consulting? Or Jennifer from auditing and assurance? Did it even matter anymore? Allison/Jennifer gave him a look so pitiful that Larry felt bad for her instead.

He stepped into the elevator and let the doors close without saying a word.

Unreal.

———

Back on the ferry, he dissected his routine. Where had it all gone wrong? Had he interrupted the space-time continuum by doing something? By *not* doing something? Was it because he drank his second cup of coffee at home instead of supporting the local café? Had he tapped the escalator rail twice instead of three times before sliding off at the top like he did every single damn time he ascended?

Dumb. All of it dumb. As much as he wanted to blame something, anything that was amiss in his daily routine, he came to the frustrating conclusion that his job situation, like everything else in life, was out of his control.

He saw his condo floor plan in his mind's eye. So much for his plan to pay off his kingdom earlier.

Kingdom, schmingdom.

But he didn't think it. He said it out loud. "Kingdom, schmingdom."

A woman nearby gave him a worried glance, then changed seats.

Damn it. All his tics were back in town.

He must have said "Damn it" aloud as well. This time, an older gentleman got up and walked to a new seat a few rows down.

Larry sighed. He needed his fix.

It was time to visit Sunil Datta.

Chapter 3

The Bay Street Mini Mart was one of those gas station/ convenience store hybrids that had popped up everywhere on Staten Island in the last few years. Once the site of a used car dealership, the Datta family had bought the dilapidated little garage a few years back, renovated it, and transformed it into a money-making machine. Larry would have killed to do their taxes.

When he went to the Bay Street Mini Mart to buy milk, the occasional snack, or that flavored seltzer Sarah liked, he walked. It was about half a mile there and back; nothing too major. He counted it as exercise. But today, he didn't want to risk anyone he knew seeing him out and about during the workday—especially Sarah. She was supposed to go see a client in New Jersey today, but he didn't know what time she needed to leave. When he saw that her car was gone from her assigned spot next to his, a wave of relief washed over him. He opened the door to his SUV and collapsed into the driver's seat. He reached into the glove compartment, pulled out a Mets hat, stuck it on his head, and pulled it down low on his forehead.

As he turned into the parking lot, he saw that it was business as usual at the Bay Street Mini Mart. Out front, half a dozen cars were gassing up at the self-serve pumps and two more were waiting. Cha ching. New Jersey had it all wrong by insisting on full-service gas pumps. Why pay an attendant to pump gas when customers could do it themselves? On the far side of the lot, there were air pumps and heavy-duty car vacs, all of which, to Larry's chagrin, still required quarters to operate. People didn't carry cash with them these days, let alone quarters. A narrow, paved driveway led back to an automatic car wash that served a constant stream of traffic most days.

He walked into the store and heard a little *bing bong* that alerted the staff when someone was there. A needless touch because someone was always in the store, buying candy, snacks, windshield wiper fluid, a cup of coffee, or lottery tickets.

So many lottery tickets.

When Larry had heard how much money a store could bring in by way of lottery tickets, he considered whether he and Sarah should install a ticket machine in their living room. Their building was full of well-funded retirees, and boy, did they love to gamble. Most weekends, about half their neighbors headed to Atlantic City, so he'd figured he was onto something.

But Sarah declined, saying a lottery machine didn't mesh well with their condo's decor. She also wasn't keen on getting involved with running a gambling operation. But he didn't think of it that way. Yes, you had to pay to play. And it was also true that you would lose that payment more often than not. But he still did not consider himself a gambling man. Gamblers went to casinos, where they made multiple trips back and forth between the ATM machine and the tables or slot machines. They made rash decisions that often ended up with empty wallets and unhappy spouses. No, he was no gambler. He was an *investor*. But unlike investors who played the stock market, he reserved his extra cash for scratch-off cards from the New York Lottery.

Larry's investment of choice was a four-by-five-inch scratch-off card called Made in the Shade. This slim little card offered a top payment of three thousand dollars a week for life. He liked this one because even after taxes were taken out of the prize money, the winner was still left with an annual six-figure payout. A very good salary for most people. Not bad for the daunting task of uncovering three matching beach umbrellas with a few scrapes of a coin.

Of course, he was no dummy. He knew there were higher paying games out there. Much higher. The current Power Payday jackpot was in "stupid money" territory, as his friend Dougie would say. Four hundred and eighty million dollars and climbing, if the bus stop ads were to be believed. Way too much. Larry approved of prize amounts that would set the winner up for this lifetime, not twelve. He wasn't that greedy.

That's why he chose to invest his allotted twenty dollars per week on Made in the Shade. Just a single bill from an ATM withdrawal. He paid for most things with plastic, but by New York State law, lottery ticket purchases must be made in cash. He had no problem forking it over to a cheerful Sunil. Besides, twenty dollars was far less than what he would spend on lunch each week if he didn't take a sandwich to work.

No, twenty dollars a week was not a problem, and it was not an obsession. Nothing to see here, folks! The scratch-off cards were a mindless habit he had picked up soon after September 11, when New York City was piecing itself back together and he was feeling lucky to be alive.

One morning on his way to work, back when he was a fresh-faced young man of twenty-two, Larry had come out of the subway station and found a dollar on the ground. He picked it up with the intention of giving it to some homeless person on his way to his office, but that day there was not one in sight.

He found himself, still with the dollar in hand, in front of the convenience store around the corner from his office where he often stopped to get a cheap (but good) cup of coffee. He shrugged his shoulders and walked in.

A clerk was refilling the coffee urns. "Fresh coffee in five."

Maybe he'd buy a pack of gum and drink the coffee at the office instead.

He got in line and eyed the candy rack, looking for the brand of spearmint gum he liked. Ahead of him was an older woman wearing a bright pink velour jogging suit and carrying an expensive-looking purse. She smiled at him, her lips the same color as her outfit. In her hand was a stack of lottery scratch-off cards. When it was her turn, she handed the clerk the stack and folded her hands on the counter to wait while he scanned each card.

Larry stared in awe. With each blip of the scanner, a computerized bugle sound declared the glad tidings of the winning ticket. The woman's cards were all winners.

"Hundred fifty," the cashier said. He looked bored. Larry would learn later that convenience store clerks hated it when the scratch-off players came in this early in the day because they would cash in their winnings and leave the store with very little money in the till. But this woman wasn't interested in cash. She nodded when the cashier confirmed her earnings, then she took out a slip of paper. She glanced down and read off her notes.

"Ten number fives, five number eights, and five number twenties. Oh, and ten number threes." The cashier walked over to the plastic case with the numbered rolls. He counted out her cards and handed the stack to the woman with a slight bow. She nodded.

Larry wondered if the lady would go home and scratch them off all at once or if she would linger over them for a while, maybe scratching a few each day, a kind of delayed gratification.

She took her cards, turned around, and glided past him. There was a look in her eye, something he couldn't quite pinpoint. Anticipation? Greed? Triumph? He couldn't tell. All he knew was he was standing there with a dollar in his hand.

The cashier looked at him and raised an eyebrow.

He scanned the card case, searching for a card that cost a dollar.

"Um, I'll take a number twelve."

The cashier tore off the card and handed it to him. "Good luck."

That was nice of him to say, though it made Larry feel silly. In the grand scheme of the lottery world, those small cards were the equivalent of penny slot machines. For the same amount, he could buy a lottery ticket for the multimillion-dollar prize and take a chance on something big. Or he could just save his hard-earned money for a down payment on a home one of these years.

He stared down at the card, mumbled his thanks, and walked out of the store. He searched his pockets for a coin and found a dime. He stood under an awning and turned toward the building for some semblance of privacy. He placed the card in the palm of his left hand, pinched the slender dime between his right thumb and index finger, and began scratching.

About ten seconds later, he uncovered two matching numbers and a dollar sign. He was a winner! Of what, he wasn't sure.

He squinted down at the card to read the fine print regarding the prize. Boom. He had won another card. So that's how they pulled you in.

He went back into the store with the express purpose of getting coffee this time. He walked over to the self-serve station, poured himself a small paper cup of steaming hot Colombian roast that had just finished brewing, and dumped in a tiny cup of cream. He swirled a stirrer through the steaming liquid and snapped a lid on the cup. He went back up to the counter, where there was yet another person buying scratch-off tickets.

He paid the buck fifty for his coffee with a five-dollar bill. He popped the two quarters in the donation jar on the counter for a local animal shelter. Then, he handed the remaining three dollars plus the winning card to the cashier.

"Four number twelves, please." He made his voice sound authoritative. This was no big deal. He was already a natural. Face expressionless, the cashier wished him luck again, and it was on to the next customer.

Larry returned to his spot beneath the awning and reached into his pocket again for the dime. He placed his coffee cup on the sidewalk between his feet and scratched the silver coating from the cards, a surge of excitement bubbling in his gut.

Two dollars on one card, nothing on another, and then he won a new card on each of the remaining cards. He tucked the winners away in an inner pocket in his bag and made himself promise to wait at least a week before cashing them in. He could see how easy it was to get carried away with it all. But that wasn't his style. This scratch-off thing was a passing phase, like that one summer during college when he dabbled in protein shakes and lifting weights. It wouldn't last.

—

The owner of the Bay Street Mini Mart, Sunil Datta, looked up from behind the counter at the *bing bong* signaling Larry's entrance. Sunil was a friendly man whose thick mane of gray hair was the sole betrayal of his age. He gave Larry a gracious nod. This was good. He'd been hoping that Sunil would be behind the counter and not his son, Gaurav, who was a lanky replica of his dad, except with a shock of black hair and a bad attitude. Perhaps this transaction would be easy after all.

If he were stopping by to pick up milk or a cup of coffee and the newspaper, Larry could go about his normal business, maybe even say hello to someone he knew from the neighborhood who also happened to be there. But when he was there to buy his scratch-off tickets, there was a strict procedure to follow.

He walked to the newspaper rack and picked up a copy of the *Staten Island Advance*.

He went to the refrigerated section and got a bottle of iced tea.

He went into the candy and snack aisle. He didn't have much of an appetite, but procedure was procedure.

He picked up a package of chocolate cupcakes. With his requisite three items in hand, he took a deep breath and walked up to stand in the short line at the counter.

When it was his turn, he said "Good morning" in a voice much lower and deeper than normal. He wanted to sound mysterious, but he was sure it sounded more like he was getting a cold.

"Mr. Larry! You are here early this week."

Larry's nostrils twitched. Perhaps he was getting a cold after all. He cleared his throat.

Sunil looked remorseful. "I mean, good to see you after not being here in such a long time."

Larry gave a tight smile, reaching into his back pocket and for his wad of scratch-off cards. Last week's haul had been a good one. He placed the pile on the counter, then added a crisp twenty to it, fresh from the ATM. He cleared his throat again, and in the deepest voice he could muster, said, "Fifteen number nines, please."

Sunil smiled and reached for the roll of tickets.

The door to the small office behind the counter opened, and, to Larry's dismay, Gaurav emerged. Sunil's son was around twenty-five but had the maturity of a high schooler. He looked at Larry in disdain. Gaurav looked at everyone in disdain. He'd graduated from an MBA program last spring and had yet to find a job in finance, so he worked at his father's store.

Gaurav shifted his sharp gaze to Larry's Mets hat. "Aren't you a Yankees fan?"

Larry picked up the newspaper and scanned the front page.

But Gaurav would not be ignored. "Yes, you are. Why the Mets hat? Is it your disguise?"

"What do you mean?" Larry's voice cracked. His hand reached out and tapped the counter, making the pennies in the charity jar rattle.

Gaurav laughed. "Dude, they are scratch-off tickets, not heroin."

He was right. Larry could stop at any time.

Sunil, finished with counting thirty tickets, tore them off the roll.

"Where did you come from, rude boy! Not from me. Not from your kind mama. Get out of here and go alphabetize the candies."

Gaurav walked away, chuckling.

"I am so sorry, Mr. Larry. My son is an idiot." Sunil gave him his tickets in a small brown bag.

Larry waved his hand as if to say "no he's not." But yes, Gaurav was indeed an idiot.

"See you next week." Larry was back to using his normal voice. He folded the small bag and slid it into his pocket. Then he got the hell out of there.

Instead of pulling into his assigned parking spot, he continued around to the visitors' lot on the far side of his building. He wanted to avoid any neighbors seeing him back home in the middle of the workday.

He parked and turned off the car. He reached into the center console for the pair of cheap sunglasses he got as a promotion last summer at Yankee Stadium and slid them on. Yes, his Mets hat had been sort of a disguise—he was indeed a Yankees fan—but Gaurav's taunts had rattled him. He needed a better cover next time.

He took his lucky *lira* from the cup holder. On the last day of his study abroad program in Rome, he'd had two Italian coins left in his pocket—this one and another that he'd flung over his shoulder into the Trevi Fountain. He believed in the local legend, that anyone who tossed a coin into the fountain would return to Rome one day. So much for destiny. He couldn't even use this coin anymore if he ever went back. Italy had used the euro for years now. He remembered his expired passport and sighed.

Then, he began his ritual.

He stretched the scratch-offs like an accordion. He detached each one with a satisfying tear and put the stack in the cup holder. He chose one at random, placed it on the center of his steering wheel, and scraped the coin against the coating on the card.

The first card—no prize. There was nothing on the second one, either. Third one didn't even come close.

He set his jaw and took another card from the pack. His hand was already starting to cramp in the cold, so he switched the coin to his left hand and went back to work.

He flinched when the car's horn honked under the pressure. He moved the card to the dashboard and continued. At last, he uncovered one of the beach umbrellas. He'd won another card. Good. He shook off the silver dust into his half-empty coffee cup and placed the winner on the passenger seat.

He found two umbrellas on the next card, which netted him eight dollars. He was still down money from the other two duds. He swiped at his forehead with the back of his hand. He was sweating. He needed to hit something soon to recoup his investment.

Then, he hit pay dirt on the last card—an umbrella with a dollar sign on it. Twenty-five bucks.

He leaned back in his seat and exhaled. He took out a tiny notebook and pen from his console, turned the pages until he found an empty line, then wrote down his winnings for the week: Thirty-three dollars. He'd started a tally when his game play got serious about ten years ago. The win/loss ratio went up and down, up and down. But the past two years had been a pretty good run for him. All told, he was up by around forty-five hundred dollars.

He flung the notebook aside, then the pen. It was not enough to pay off the mortgage. It was never going to be enough, certainly not now that his job was gone. His partial kingdom would remain just that—partial.

He was going to have to—

Thwack.

He slammed his foot on the brake, even though the car's ignition was off.

A man, who either didn't see Larry or else didn't care, had lifted the car's windshield wiper to insert a flyer, then let it slam down. People still did that? How annoying.

He opened his door enough to reach out his left arm and snatched the flyer.

FILING YOUR TAXES IS EASY
AT ISLAND TAX PREP
NOW HIRING TAX PREPARERS
NO ACCOUNTING EXPERIENCE REQUIRED
WE WILL TRAIN YOU!!!

He snorted.

He looked closer at the phone number and email address at the bottom of the neon green page, the same color as his highlighter.

27 percent.

No. No way in hell. He was better than working at the neighborhood tax firm. Four years of college, plus an extra year for an accelerated graduate program. A summer of intensive study for the CPA exam. More than fifteen years of spreadsheets. And yet here he was. Unemployed.

He tucked his scratch-offs away in the center console and grabbed his phone. He tapped the steering wheel three times, exhaled, and then tapped in the phone number from the flyer.

Chapter 4

The Island Tax Prep office was in a small strip mall on Victory Boulevard about a mile from the condo. He had passed the place millions of times and never noticed it, as often happened when he had no interest in or need for something. Gyms and fitness centers were invisible to him for that very reason.

He parked at the far end of the lot and walked down the sidewalk in the shadow of the stores' awnings. He glanced into each window as he went by. A Chinese take-out place with a staff bustling around, preparing for the lunchtime rush. A small market with wilting produce in the window. A nail salon, but the sign said it was closed on Mondays. At the end of the strip, there was an empty storefront. A sign in the store window said VARMA'S CONVENIENCE STORE COMING SOON.

Next door to the soon-to-be convenience store was Island Tax Prep. Larry walked into the vestibule and was greeted by an empty reception desk. He lost his nerve and turned to leave, but a man appeared.

"Are you Larry? I'm Irving, the office manager." This was

the pleasant-sounding guy who picked up the phone when he called. Irving had a firm handshake and a smile that revealed teeth so white, it reminded Larry that he had to call HR to see about how to extend his medical and dental benefits. He'd just been for a physical, but it had been ages since he'd gone for a cleaning.

Larry forced a smile and a handshake and accepted a clipboard with an application.

"Take your time filling that out, then come to my office in the back when you're ready," Irving said.

It didn't take Larry long to fill out the application. That was the good thing about having worked at one company for so long. But it did pain him to see that fifteen years of his life could be summed up in just a few lines.

Larry took a seat on one side of an ancient green metal desk in Irving's office. He was trying his best not to look humiliated. He tried to sit up straight, but he kept slouching, like a human sack of potatoes. He looked at his watch. 11:30. How on earth was it still Monday morning?

Irving's forehead crinkled as he read Larry's application. He seemed concerned.

"You're a CPA?"

"That's right."

"Sooooo, a *real* accountant, are you?"

"Yes."

"We don't have many of those around here."

Larry didn't know how to respond to that.

"All of our employees completed our crash course in tax preparation. Two hours, two nights a week for four weeks. They learned everything from a W-2 form to, you know, all the other forms the IRS needs. In brief, of course."

The two men nodded at each other.

"You saw our flyer?" Irving's smile was back.

"Couldn't miss it."

Irving launched into how they were here to serve the tax

needs of the community. Something about wanting to be a friendly, welcoming place so people didn't dread April 15 so much. Larry peered around the vertical blinds in the office window and scoped out his future coworkers. There was a woman filing her nails at one desk. At another, an older woman was knitting some tube-like garment. Perhaps it was a sock or a sleeve to a sweater, but judging by the number of dog statues crowding the woman's desk, he guessed it could also be the start of a tiny dog's sweater. One man was playing solitaire with an actual deck of cards. A man who looked to be in his early to mid-twenties was engrossed in a thick textbook.

"Judging by your experience, of course, you could teach the course."

"Thank you." Larry smiled. Then his cheek twitched.

Irving's eyebrows drew together into a look of pity. "Got laid off, huh?"

Larry blinked twice. His right foot twitched three times. He stared at his hands and nodded.

What else was he supposed to do?

Rick was right. Accounting firm mergers were happening all over town. How many other CPAs were doing their own professional walk of shame right now? No firm was going to pick him up now. Even if they did, the onboarding process would take all tax season. He didn't want to go on unemployment. He didn't want to tell Sarah and have her freak out about how much he'd have to pay to keep their healthcare benefits in the meantime. He was ashamed to reach out to his professional network for help, though he knew he would have to if he wanted a good position somewhere. The idea of sending his résumé through the black vortex of job boards like he was a twenty-something nobody was repugnant.

But the truth was even worse. Larry was a thirty-something nobody. So, when Irving offered him the job, Larry accepted.

A half hour later, Larry was sitting at an empty desk reading the Island Tax Prep manual. Textbook Guy, who had gone to lunch, returned to the office with his phone wedged in between his ear and shoulder. He carried a bottle of soda in one hand and a pen and pad in the other. "Uh huh. Yep. Uh huh." He smiled and flashed Larry an index finger. "One minute," he mouthed.

Larry gave a small salute and resumed reading the manual.

A few minutes and about a dozen "uh huhs" and "yeps" later, the guy ended his call and spun around in his squeaky chair, almost falling out of it in the process. He took it in stride and righted himself with a smile.

"You our new man?"

"Larry Sortino."

They shook hands.

"I'm Jordan Brunner." He made his voice sound a bit like a newscaster on TV. "What do you do?"

"I'm an accountant."

"Right, we're all *accountants*." He made quotation marks with his fingers.

"No, I'm a CPA."

"Oh, you got laid off?"

Larry's knee twitched three times, the third time hitting the underside of the metal desk.

Jordan winced. "That's going to leave a mark."

Larry shook his head. "What do you do, Jordan?"

Jordan took a deep breath. "What don't I do?"

Oh boy.

"Well, I do this." Jordan gestured at the office with a flourish. "I tend bar on the weekends. And I flip couches."

"Wow, you flip houses?" Jordan was tall, skinny, and didn't look at all athletic. He didn't strike Larry as someone who would be proficient with any kind of power tool.

"Not houses, couches. I buy couches and loveseats cheap, then I throw them in the back of my pickup truck, drive to the Village, and sell them to the kids at NYU."

"Ah."

"I'm also studying to be a TV news reporter." Jordan

pointed to his textbook, something about speech or mass communications.

"Well, your elevator pitch is on point," Larry said. "When do you graduate?"

"Oh, I'm not in a degree program. I'm just taking a couple of media classes at the College of Staten Island. There's a news writing course I'm trying to get in over the summer. It's what I can afford right now. I moved back home for a bit. My mom—"

"Oh. Hey, that's great." Larry sensed Jordan's embarrassment. "I mean, that you're able to take care of your mom."

Jordan opened his mouth as if he were going to say something. Instead, he smiled and nodded.

"Hey, good luck, man."

"Right. Um, thanks." Jordan spun back around to face his desk.

Irving opened his office door and called to Larry.

"I borrowed a desk," Larry said.

"That's fine. Let's discuss your hours."

Larry joined him in his office. Irving motioned for him to close the door, then he leaned in.

"Now don't let this get out. Because you're the real McCoy, management says I can give you a buck fifty an hour more than the others."

Chapter 5

It was a good thing that Dougie and Sarah got along so well. Or at least that's what Larry used to think.

He bought very much into the greeting card version of marriage: Sarah was his wife, his lover, and his best friend. But the sentiment didn't mean either of them had to give the heave-ho to any of their existing friends. It made life fuller, he believed, that his buddies would become her buddies and her gal pals would become his.

But as the years passed, his buddies got whittled down to a singular buddy—Dougie Teague. The last friend standing. Dougie didn't have a wife or kids. He bought a smaller condo in the building across the parking lot from theirs. Sarah was at ease around him, comfortable in calling out his silly habits, of which there were so many. "You're a buffoon," she would often tell him. A more practiced eye than Larry's might have detected the trace of a smile despite herself.

Sarah's girlfriends moved to other parts of the city, where they settled down with spouses and, a bit later, kids. They had all downloaded one of those virtual conference call apps to keep in touch. Never one to sit still for long, she would run around the apartment with her phone bobbing in front of her face as she chattered away with Abby, Melissa, and Christina—or maybe it was Laura. He was never good with telling the difference between the twins.

Larry would peek over Sarah's shoulder and wave at the ladies, their pictures displayed on her screen in a way that always reminded him of the opening credits of *The Brady Bunch*. Often, she and her friends would have those ridiculous photo filters hovering over their images. Abby had dog ears and a long tongue that lapped whenever she opened her mouth, Melissa had bunny ears and a twitching nose, and Christina/Laura looked like a cat. Sarah had added a unicorn horn to her own image. For some reason that one made sense to Larry.

Talking on the phone was one thing, but getting together in person had proved difficult for Sarah. Abby moved way uptown, Melissa was in a part of Brooklyn that took two different subways to get to, and Christina/Laura moved out to Long Island. It was too crazy of a commute for coffee or cocktails anymore.

Her social circle had also shrunk. Nothing to be done. There was nothing malicious about the transformation, of course, no hard feelings, but distance and evolving family situations had given Sarah the short end of the stick when it came to sustaining her friendships.

One Saturday morning after his shower, Larry sat in his robe on their bed and scrolled through his social media feed. He had a love-hate relationship with social media—it kept him in touch with the news, but it also made him privy to the most mundane details of his friends' and acquaintances' lives. A time suck for sure. But he had nowhere to go that day, so he figured he'd kill some time while he waited for Sarah to return from her run.

He scrolled to a picture of Sarah's friends, Abby, Melissa, and Christina, with their kids all tucked into their age-appropriate strollers or carriers. The happy group was smiling in the sunshine at the entrance of the Central Park Zoo.

He winced. Had Sarah seen it? He looked below the photo and saw that Sarah had tapped the like button. She even added a comment, though it was just a series of smile and heart emojis.

His heart swelled with love for his wife. She could have ignored the post, not commented at all. But he knew she wouldn't let her disappointment of being left out of motherhood get in the way of her friendships. He wondered if he should say anything about it. This was his beef with social media—it often brought an unnecessary layer of complication to his real-world relationships.

He got dressed and went into the living room. He was surprised to see Sarah curled up on the couch, dressed in her workout gear, sniffling as she swiped at her phone screen.

Without a word, he sat down next to her and put a hand on her knee. She sighed and put her hand on his. They sat like that for a while, not moving, not speaking. Then she got up, kissed him, and left for her run.

The doctors had no definitive answers as to why she couldn't get pregnant. Both of them were the picture of health for thirty-eight-year-olds. He had submitted to a battery of tests, but they all came back negative for whatever it was they were looking for. Yes, she was considered a "geriatric mother" at her age, but her tests showed nothing conclusive, either. They were just another couple in the "unexplained infertility" column and soon-to-be recipients of a lifetime of pity from those with children—or at least that's what she said to him through shaking sobs on the way home from the doctor's office.

But they'd kept trying. Having more sex with his beautiful wife wasn't exactly a chore. He had always been monogamous by nature, but when he began dating Sarah fifteen years ago, he lost his ability to find other women attractive. He saw the institution of marriage as a sacred pact, although he hadn't made an appearance in church in some time.

Still, the pact was starting to show signs of wear. He tried to pinpoint when things started to fall apart between them, but he couldn't be sure, which was maddening. It might have been around the time when their conversations devolved into simple phrases and one-word answers. Although they shared a king bed, they kept to their own opposite sides, their limbs never daring to strain toward the middle where they might touch. He imagined they were like the couple in that mattress commercial, which demonstrated how the king-size mattress was large enough to offer complete comfort despite their preferred sleeping positions. For the record, he was often on his back, fingers laced on his belly, and she was on her side, curled up in the fetal position.

At the same time he was disconnecting from Sarah, he was also drifting further away from Dougie. This, at first, was even more hurtful, but it did make a lot more sense. When a friendship starts because of adolescent hobbies like playing Dungeons and Dragons and reading comic books, things were bound to change over time. Larry still read the latest volumes of the superheroes, but his trips to the comic book store were replaced by ordering them online and having them delivered to his doorstep in padded manila envelopes. Dougie much preferred watching the game—any game—on television rather than reading these days.

But that's how it went, right? As people grew older, their careers—Larry, accounting; Dougie, construction—took them further and further away from their shared experiences until there was nothing that kept them in each other's lives except routine and a stubbornness not to bend from that routine.

Sarah and Dougie were sleeping together behind his back, of course. When he finally figured out that Sarah's frequent runs took her on a route through the parking lot to Dougie's place, he was embarrassed that it had taken him so long. He'd thought he had better powers of deduction. After all, he had gotten his start in forensic accounting. He knew fraud when he saw it. People might try to hide, but numbers bared themselves. They couldn't lie. But, apparently, the heart could. At least, for a while.

It was his mother's refrain—"Numbers don't lie, but people do." She would say it when the alimony check from his dad arrived in the mail. It wasn't a bitter sentiment, just a truth that Diane Sortino believed in with all her might. It was a proud day when, after a couple of years, his mother put a stop to those pity checks, as she called them. She signed the contract from her lawyer with a flourish, affirming they would no longer need any financial support from Larry Sortino, Sr..

It took Larry even longer to admit to himself that he was not devastated by Sarah and Dougie's shenanigans. Perhaps he was able to take it in stride because there wasn't much of an audience to witness his cuckolding. They had some of the most aloof neighbors ever. There was little threat of any "tsk, tsks," no well-meaning glances or snide remarks that would alert him to the infidelity. No one was curious about how the Sortinos or anyone else lived their lives. It was one of the reasons they loved living in their building.

He was loath to think about it all. He did love his wife. But was he still *in* love with her? Could they still be happy together? The matter was up for a debate that neither of them seemed willing to have. As for Dougie, he couldn't stomach the sight of him anymore, but he didn't have the courage to say anything.

He wanted Sarah to be happy, that much he knew. But he didn't know how to make her happy anymore, which was both a surprise and a disappointment to him. Then again, those were the same emotions he experienced with his scratch-off cards. Perhaps that meant he felt nothing at all.

Chapter 6

"I'm so sorry. It was a mistake."

The regret in Sarah's voice was sincere.

They peered into their refrigerator, staring at the empty shelf where there should have been milk. It was on the shopping list, but she'd forgotten to pick it up. His morning coffee ritual was in peril. He could drink it black, but he craved the routine of that half a glug of milk now more than ever.

"No worries. I'll walk to the store."

"It's freezing out, Lah." Despite growing up in Bay Ridge, Sarah didn't have a heavy New York accent. But when she called him Lah, it sounded like blaahh, as if she were kicking the letter R out of the alphabet with her tongue.

"I'm sure I'll live."

He took his coat from the hall closet and put it on, then tugged on a hat and a pair of gloves. He reached into his pocket to check for the winning scratch-offs from earlier and left the condo.

Of course, it wasn't about the milk. It was never about the

milk. It was always about those damn scratch-off cards. And it started long before he ever found that lucky dollar on the street.

It started with his mother.

Diane Sortino's primary calling was to teach math to fourth graders. She preferred students before their hormones kicked in. It was fulfilling for her to be a part of the daily lives of hundreds of fourth graders over the years and their quest to master word problems and long division. But she was in her element during summer vacations and holiday breaks when she worked as a local sales representative for a big makeup and skin care product company.

"I wipe off the chalk dust, and I dust on some bronzing powder," she would say when introducing herself to the ladies at the in-home skin care parties she hosted. She rehearsed her pitch to Larry at the kitchen table, who was a captive audience despite his complete lack of interest in what she had to sell. He didn't understand her joke, of course, though she assured him that line was a hit with the housewife crowd.

What did enthrall him was watching his mother become a different person. To say his mother was good at selling makeup would be to say the sun was bright or grass was green. Maybe it was her good genes that created her glowing complexion that the other ladies coveted. Maybe it was the fact that the cosmetics and skin care products she sold were as good as they were advertised to be. But when Diane Sortino stood before the lady of the house and her assorted friends and acquaintances at each of those little parties, her sales pitch slayed. At 50 percent commission, she was able to match her teacher's salary that first year and double it the second.

But it was more than just selling lipstick. She was recruiting for her own sales team. That's how you made real money in multilevel marketing. After each party, she would come home with a zippered case full of cash and checks, as well as the phone numbers of women who were interested in learning more about how they, too, could do what Diane Sortino did.

Her ascent in sales began in the 1980s, when hair was big and makeup was heavy and bright. She herself preferred a more modest look, but that didn't stop her customers from buying doubles of their favorite lipsticks, lip liners, and eye shadows. At her local sales team's weekly meetings, she was often crowned Queen of Sales, a plastic tiara placed on her dark bob by her beaming sales director. As she built her team and continued to sell, those incredible, almost mythical multilevel marketing commission levels kicked in.

Diane Sortino was on her way up, far up in the makeup world. She earned the jewelry and trips and even the cars to prove it. Did Larry care that his mother drove him to school in a lavender sedan? No sir, because no one else's mom had a car that started up each and every time, not to mention one that was paid off.

That's how it was for years and years. When she was convinced that he had learned enough arithmetic in grade school, he was tasked with his mother's bookkeeping. He saw her sales figures start to add up, grew wide-eyed when he saw the cash flow. Until then, he hadn't been interested in money. He asked his mother why she would bother anymore with teaching when it was clear she could make even more money in sales.

"What if a competitor comes along and wipes out my business, Larry?" she said, kissing him on the top of his head. "Besides, I'm not giving up my teacher pension."

One night after a sales meeting, she came home, awash in a light scent of a brand-new fragrance released just in time for the holidays. She had been recognized as Queen of Sales once again, but instead of a free lipstick and the plastic tiara (it had cracked in half when it got stuck in another salesperson's stiffly sprayed coif the week before), she was gifted with a short stack of lottery scratch-off tickets.

She sat down at the kitchen table, a quarter squeezed between her thumb and forefinger, ready to determine her fate. He watched, intrigued by his mother's giggles as she scratched away. With a few firm scrapes of the quarter's edge, she swept away the silver layer to uncover prizes that could amount to anything: a can of soda, the grocery bill, maybe even the mortgage payment. Of course, it could also turn out to be nothing at all, which was true for two of the cards. When this happened, she sighed.

"Wouldn't it be nice ..." Her voice trailed off.

But when he asked her what would be nice, she didn't answer.

His mom won twenty-five dollars that first time. Beginner's luck, of course, but she was thrilled and grateful. Now she had Larry's lunch money for two whole weeks. She went to the convenience store around the corner and cashed in the cards, getting him a candy bar while she was at it. That Monday morning, she gave him a twenty-dollar bill plus a five-dollar bill that she pulled from the cookie jar. She smiled.

"Giving you five of mine."

He peered into the jar to see a narrow stack of new scratch-off cards. He looked back at his mom, eyebrows raised.

"I reinvested a little." She shrugged.

From that point on, there would always be scratch-off tickets in the cookie jar. The possibility of spending a little and getting a lot never grew old. The New York Lottery had gotten under Diane Sortino's well-moisturized skin.

It got under Larry's as well.

—

There was a traffic jam at the gas pumps. A row of cars lined the back roadway leading to the car wash. Larry squinted. There were no drivers in any of the cars. There was an eerie silence. It seemed like the opening credits of that zombie television series Sarah was fond of watching.

As he got closer, he was relieved to see that one of the cars did have a driver in it. The guy got out of his car and yelled to no one in particular, "Can I just get my frickin' car washed?"

Larry looked to the front of the store and was surprised to see a line had formed outside the door. Some people were stamping their feet to stay warm. Others were staring at their phones. None looked like they wanted to feast on his brains. Still confused, but feeling an odd sense of relief, he joined the back of the line.

There was an older couple in front of him. The man turned around and nodded. He accepted it as a chance to ask what in the hell was going on.

"Is there a snowstorm coming?" He willed his voice to sound casual. He never was much for small talk. He made a mental note to grab a loaf of bread with his milk. That is, if there was still any left.

"Power Payday," the man said.

"Oh, the lottery. Is it a big one?"

The man's eyes widened.

"Hell yeah. No one has won it for three weeks now. Up over five hundred."

His wife, or maybe it was his "lady friend," turned around. She looked like the woman from the paper towel commercial he remembered from when he was a kid. He wondered what Sarah would look like when she got to her age, whatever that might be. He was always terrible at guessing people's ages.

"Actually, it's five hundred seventy-five."

"Wow. Million?"

"Have you been living under a rock?" the woman asked.

"Oh. I, uh, don't play."

The couple looked horrified, then offended. They turned back around.

Larry sighed. He had some very high-net-worth tax clients, but five hundred and seventy-five million dollars was astronomical. He could crunch impressive figures, but he never liked it when the numbers went that sky-high. From a practical perspective, there wasn't enough room to fit figures like that on a calculator screen, and he needed to make far too many adjustments to fit them into a spreadsheet. Besides, what on earth would the winner do with all that money? That's why he stuck with his scratch-off tickets. At least those prize amounts didn't give him a migraine. Excitement delivered in doable doses. That was what he liked.

In a few minutes, he was inside the store. Sunil and Gaurav were bustling around, smiling as they collected cash and handed out tickets. Well, at least Sunil was smiling. Gaurav looked ready for a fight.

Dammit. He scratched his head, tugging at a spot where just that morning he saw a gray hair had popped up among the dark brown. All he wanted was to cash in his few scratch-offs and pocket the pitiful thirty-three dollars that he had won that week. But there were too many people in the store. Too many eyes to watch him indulge in the one diversion he had to break up the monotony of his days. He might as well have been standing there naked. He would have to find another hobby (not an obsession) that didn't make him feel so ashamed.

The line was moving again. He wanted to deal with Sunil, but Gaurav waved him over. "Hey, next customer!"

He walked up to the counter. He didn't even bother with the authoritative voice this time. "Five number eights, please."

Gaurav pointed to the plastic containers of scratch-off cards.

He assumed Gaurav hadn't heard him.

"Five number eights, please," he said, louder this time.

Gaurav jabbed a finger at the containers again.

Larry saw there were number sixes and number sevens, even number nines, which were always so popular.

But there were no number eights.

He fought back a shudder.

"All your babies are gone." Gaurav pouted for effect.

Larry's head ached. Chills ran through his entire body. Was there such a thing as stress-induced flu? He got his shot back in November, but he knew there were always those people who got sick anyway. Maybe he was one of the unlucky ones.

Sunil looked over and smiled. He saw the empty number eight box and a look of alarm spread over his face.

"Mr. Larry, I am so sorry." His tone sounded like someone had died.

Gaurav grabbed a Power Payday ticket form and a golf pencil and slid it across the counter. "Here. Pick numbers. Like everyone else." Gaurav chuckled. "Maybe you'll be a winner."

Larry stood in the too-bright light of the store, tensing his body to keep it from twitching. It wasn't fair. Some men had a bar. He and Sarah had their cafés and restaurants over the years. But in a way—a very warped one, he would be willing to admit—this stupid convenience store was his place, his spot. What a loser. Shame warmed his body like an extra coat.

He took the little golf pencil and the ticket form with a trembling hand and walked over to the newspaper rack in the corner. He leaned against the rigid metal frame and stared at the ticket form, trying to focus on the little number bubbles swirling across the sheet.

He licked his dry lips. Milk. He couldn't forget the milk. Not after all of this. He had to keep up appearances. In a daze, he put down the pencil and paper on the stack of newspapers and walked over to the refrigerated section. He picked a half gallon of milk from the shelf without paying attention to the expiration date. Sour milk was the least of his problems.

He walked back toward the line, plucking a loaf of white bread from the bakery aisle on his way. He spotted a box of cupcakes, frosted in a shade of lavender that reminded him of his mother's car. He knew they would taste awful. Still, he grabbed the plastic box and made his way back to the newspaper rack.

The pencil and lottery card were still there, mocking him. Fine. He would buy this damn lottery ticket. So what if it was different from the normal routine that he had followed for a decade? He could buy any damn lottery ticket he wanted. Or not buy any lottery ticket. That was always an option, too. He could go home with his bread, milk, and cupcakes, and that would be that.

It was just a game.

But he would not give Gaurav the satisfaction of seeing him walk away empty-handed, disappointed because they were out of his scratch-offs. He would not have his night ruined by pieces of cardboard, or lack thereof.

His left palm itched. He scratched it with the back of the golf pencil. Sarah once told him itchy palms meant money was coming to you. Or was it that you were going to get into a fight? No, that was an itchy nose. The mere thought made his nose twitch, but he refused to scratch it.

He'd been lying when he told that couple he didn't play the lottery. But not because of his secret scratch-off cards. Over the years, the lottery jackpot would swell as it had now, and there would always be some optimistic coworker who would go around and collect a couple of bucks from everyone to buy tickets. He would hand over some singles, not wanting to miss out on the camaraderie of his office. He was certain no one believed they had a shot. He was also certain no one but him ever wondered, *If we all win and quit at the same time, who will take care of our clients?*

When the inevitable news came that they hadn't won, he was never disappointed. He was relieved. He wanted no part of winning that much money. How would he wrap his head around all those extra zeros? It was one thing when he balanced budgets for his wealthy clients, but it would be something different if the money were his. What would he do with it all? Yes, of course he'd pay his mortgage off, but he knew that was a practical man's way of thinking. Breaking into a millionaire's tax bracket would mean that he'd have the luxury of being impractical for once. Try something new for a change. Figure out what he wanted to do with the rest of his life. It all made his head hurt. He couldn't think that far ahead. That's one of the things he loved about accounting so much. It was better to think in terms of tax quarters and fiscal years, to not get too ahead of yourself.

Would he be able to quit his job if he won a ton of money? Well, yes. But then again, no. What would he do all day? Beads of sweat broke out on his forehead when he tried to think about what life would be like outside of the nine-to-five grind.

Fine, he would quit. It would be ridiculous to have that much money and not give someone else the opportunity to have a job with benefits. He would have to find something else to keep him busy, maybe start his own tax firm so he could keep working and earning.

Bingo. That was the thing he hated most about the big lottery games: No one *earned* the prize. They did nothing but choose numbers at random. No rhyme, no reason. No skills necessary, no résumé required. Getting that much money without doing something in return for it didn't sit well with him. If he were going to be a millionaire, he would prefer to work for it instead of getting a handout from the New York Lottery.

I'm a dumbass, he thought.

But he didn't think it. He said it out loud. "I'm a dumbass."

A woman in the back of the line turned around, gave him a once-over. She rolled her eyes and turned back around.

He knew from witnessing other lottery players that he could ask Gaurav or Sunil to let the computer tabulate random numbers for his ticket and be done with it. But he hated the lack of control in that method. He knew that's what most people would do, if they were feeling lucky. Or perhaps they'd use the tiny printed numbers on the back of the narrow slip of paper tucked inside a fortune cookie from their Chinese take-out.

But he was not like most people. That's why he preferred the scratch-offs. Even though he didn't have any control over the numbers and images that would reveal themselves behind the silver squares, he imagined that he could at least coax something, anything, to happen, by rubbing the edge of his coin across the card.

Soon he found himself the next customer. He stood there with his milk, bread, cupcakes, and a still-blank lottery card in hand. Gaurav stared at him like he was an idiot.

To avoid the wrath of the impatient customers behind him, Larry took his milk, bread, cupcakes, and stupid lottery card with the tiny pencil and went back to the corner of the store. He tried to ignore the buzz around him, but there was no way that was happening. He wished he could retreat to the solitude of his car, like he did with his scratch-offs. He would be able to focus on the task at hand as he sat in the driver's seat and not worry about the fear of judgment. It occurred to him that he should have been sitting in the backseat where the windows were tinted this entire time.

Was everyone staring at him? He looked around, his own eyes hot, but no. Not one person was looking at him. For once on this island packed with busybodies, everyone was minding their own business. Even Gaurav had given up on him and focused his efforts instead on the never-ending line of lottery hopefuls, all stuck in their own reveries about what they would do if they won.

One poor soul came in to buy something, but he turned away as soon as he saw the line. Then, a second later, the man shrugged his shoulders and joined the back of the line to await his turn for a shot at mega fortune.

At last, the line had shrunk down so that everyone was inside the store. The door slammed shut against the harsh January night air.

He looked at his watch. What time did the store close? There had to be a cut-off time for the lottery. Like Cinderella approaching midnight, but instead of last holdouts transforming into pumpkins, they would turn into stale bagels and cold coffee or whatever else was left over from breakfast earlier that day.

He narrowed his eyes and looked at the ticket form. It was now or never. He took his little red golf pencil and went to work.

He shaded in number 1. Why not? You had to start somewhere.

Next, he chose 18. April 18 was his and Sarah's wedding

anniversary.

He looked for 11 and colored it in for September 11.

A sour taste in his mouth, he filled in the number 45. At Parker & Rosenthal, he had worked on the forty-fifth floor. He hated the place, but old habits die hard.

He chose 8 for Yogi Berra's jersey.

He needed two more numbers. No, three. There was that goddamned bonus number to deal with, too.

His heart was racing, as if he had just completed a cardio workout. He was growing tired. Tired! For doing what? This was no pickax or shovel in his hands. This was not manual labor. It was a golf pencil.

He filled in his age—38.

He thought of his mother. They lived at 70 Crone Place. Seventy was the highest number he could play on the card, and he stabbed at the circle with the tip of his pencil.

Last number.

He gritted his teeth so hard he was sure a couple of them would snap right out of his gums.

He chose 27. Fuckity fuck fucking 27.

He slapped the ticket on the counter in triumph, the pencil rolling off the other side. He hoped Gaurav would slip on it like a banana peel.

He was willing to wait, but Sunil waved him over. Murmuring his apologies to the customers in line again, Larry handed his card to him. Sunil scanned the number form into the computer. The ticket printed out. He took it and shoved it into his pocket. Sunil rang up the milk, bread, and cupcakes. Larry placed a bill on the counter and waited for his change, which he put in his other pocket. He felt the stack of scratch-off tickets and sighed. What a waste of a walk.

Sunil wished him a good evening, but he ignored him and stalked out and across the parking lot. He walked along the sidewalk muttering to himself, then he turned the corner and broke out into a run. He was not in shape, plus he was also weighed down by a half gallon of milk. He looked over his shoulder as if he were evading a predator. He braced the cupcake box and bread against his chest so as not to crush them, and the container of milk swung like a pendulum at his side. Adrenaline propelled him, and before he knew it, he was at the foot of the driveway to his development. The men in the security booth even raised the mechanical gate for him, as if he were driving up in his SUV, not limping home, panting like a dog.

He slowed to a walk, gasping for air. The cold winter air stung his lungs. He deserved the pain for being so stupid.

He managed a nod to the doorman before getting on the elevator. He closed his eyes as it ascended to his floor. He walked to his door, counting the steps as he went. It took twenty-seven steps. Of course it did. He was doomed.

He made it inside and locked the door behind him.

He unlocked and locked the bolt three times. Okay. He was safe.

He listened for Sarah and heard the shower and her muffled singing.

He walked into the kitchen, stepping with confidence on the tiles in the part that they owned, tiptoeing on the ones that were still mortgaged. He put the milk in the fridge and placed the bread in the basket on the counter.

He opened the cupcake box, surprised to see that they survived his frantic escape. He chose one and sunk his teeth into the lavender icing and vanilla cake. He chewed it and swallowed. It was disgusting. Served him right. No food should be lavender, not even icing.

He flung open the cabinet door beneath the sink where the garbage pail was hidden and tossed in his half-eaten cupcake. He paused, then threw the entire box in as well. He would spare Sarah from this dessert abomination. He reached into his pocket, pulled out the lottery ticket, and dropped it on top of the cupcakes. He slammed the cabinet door.

That night he went to bed, angry at the world.

Chapter 7

L arry was used to long, hectic days at Parker & Rosenthal. "Downtime" was not a word in his vocabulary. Irving had warned him things would be a little slow at the start, so he made sure to pick up a copy of *The Times* on the way in to work. He'd get one at the deli down the block—the new convenience store next to the office hadn't opened just yet. He felt a little like he was cheating on the Bay Street Mini Mart, but he needed a break from Gaurav's smirk. If he was going to be idle at work, he'd take on the crossword. With a pen. He never wanted to see another pencil again.

One day, it was so slow that after he finished *The Times'* puzzle, he went back to the deli to buy the *Daily News* to tackle that puzzle, too. But they were out, so he grabbed the *Staten Island Advance* instead. Without so much as a glance at the front page, he flipped to the lifestyle section, where he found the crossword and Sudoku puzzles.

Before he could even look at the clue for one across, he saw her picture.

He looked closer. Was it really her?

Yes, it was her, all right.

"Cardinal Crest Country Club owner and hotelier Max Rossi and his wife, Monica, were the guests of honor at The Richmond Museum's annual Jupiter Ball," the caption read.

So they were. He lifted the newspaper from his desk and examined the photo.

In college, he knew her as Monica Scotto. She had bright blue eyes and long dark curls that bounced past her shoulders. She was the most beautiful girl he had ever seen, at least in person. Now, she was a beautiful woman. Her eyes seemed to sparkle even in the black-and-white photo. Her cheekbones were sharp and angular, which lent a serious expression to her face, even though she was smiling. Her outfit looked expensive. Sarah would wonder who she was wearing, or something like that.

He studied Max. He looked as ridiculous as ever. He still wore his black hair slicked back, though there was a lot less of it. Larry touched his scalp, raked his hand through his thick brown hair, and allowed himself a moment of smugness.

Perhaps it was residual stress from the lottery debacle the night before, but as he examined the photo, it quivered. Monica's head was nodding at him.

His mind wasn't playing tricks on him. Someone's finger was poking at the back of his newspaper. Right behind Monica's picture, to be exact. The poking intensified, and now it looked like Monica was bowing to him.

He lowered the newspaper to meet the owner of the finger.

"That is why you don't have dreams, my friend." Jordan still had his coat on and was carrying a mammoth cup of coffee.

"What are you talking about?" Larry liked that his coworkers had already accepted him into their fold, but he was long out of practice with the get-to-know-you-ness of being the new guy.

Jordan pointed at the newspaper. "I saw it happening. I visualized it."

He glanced at Monica's picture, then back at Jordan. What in holy hell was he getting at?

Then he got it. Jordan wasn't pointing or poking at Monica. He wasn't even able to see her photo from where he was standing. He was gesticulating at something else on the back of the page.

Larry peered around the newspaper. The lottery numbers. He exhaled and let out a chuckle as Jordan continued his rant. He folded the paper on the desk and turned his full attention to his aggravated coworker.

"Am I any richer this morning? No. In fact, I'm two whole dollars poorer," Jordan said.

Larry leaned back in his chair. He liked Jordan. But he had a growing suspicion that this tall skinny dude was one of those people who could get on your nerves, if you let him.

"That's why I don't play." Larry was surprised by his own confidence.

"Ever?"

"Nope." He made a popping sound with his lips. "Why should I? Odds of winning are absurd."

"Yeah," Jordan said. "For the loser, like a million to one. For the winner, no odds."

"No odds?"

Jordan held up his hands. "No odds. It happened." He took a moment to reflect on that bit of wisdom. He seemed pleased with himself. Then his face darkened. "You know who won? Probably some schmuck who's never played before. I guess I should be glad they're from the Island. I hate it when out-of-towners win the jackpot."

"They're from Staten Island?"

"Yeah, didn't you hear? The winning ticket was bought at some convenience store on Bay Street." Jordan let out a mean chuckle. "Bet it was a lottery virgin. Some jerk who just stopped in for milk and bread. A dumbass who can't appreciate the beauty of a seven-number combo. That glorious, unattainable bonus number." He leaned in. "Probably only ever played those pussy scratch-off tickets before."

This time, Larry's chuckle sounded more like he was choking.

But Jordan wasn't paying attention. He looked at the numbers again and groaned.

"Man, those are the worst numbers. Why can't I get lucky like that?"

Larry had nothing good to say, so he cracked open the fortune cookie from his lunch. He ignored his trembling hand. He squinted at the sliver of paper and read. "A lucky man has everything he needs and nothing he wants."

Jordan mulled that over for a few seconds. "Horseshit."

Larry laughed and handed the fortune to Jordan, who swatted it away.

"But there are lottery numbers on the back! Save them for next time."

Jordan gave him a dark look, then headed back to his desk, leaving him with his crossword.

—

Luck was a matter of opinion.

Larry hadn't considered himself a lucky guy for the first twenty-two years of his life. It's not that he was unlucky. He did have a lot to be thankful for. But he didn't believe that amazing things ever happened to regular Joes like him.

That idea changed on September 11, 2001. He had graduated that May and started a full-time job with the auditing team at Parker & Rosenthal. His first client was a marketing firm on the fiftieth floor of One World Trade Center. On that Tuesday, he woke up with such insane sinus pressure that he couldn't move his head without groaning. He was used to seasonal allergies, but this was real pain. He found temporary comfort lying across his bed with his head hanging downward, gasping through his mouth.

He grabbed his brand-new cell phone and left a message with Valerie, his team lead, that he wouldn't be in that day.

He swallowed two aspirin with a glass of water from the tap and fell back into bed. An hour later, he awoke with a jolt. He stared at the TV. The images he saw on the screen didn't make sense. A skyscraper on fire. No, make that two skyscrapers. People running down the street, eyes darting all around, their faces contorted by confusion and fear. A somber look on the newscaster's face.

He rolled over for a closer look. Had he switched channels? Was this one of those crazy disaster movies? He looked at his cellphone and saw the voicemail alert blinking.

No, this was still *The Today Show*. Something terrible was going on.

And then he saw one of the Twin Towers fall.

His phone vibrated and he flipped it open.

"Hello?"

"Thank God. Oh Joan, he's alive." His mother. He heard her sob, and the murmur of the school secretary in the background.

Diane Sortino was not one to cry. She loved her son more than anything in this world, but she wasn't dramatic about it. This level of emotion was new.

"Ma, what the hell?"

"Oh, it's awful, just awful."

He listened as she rattled off names. "You're okay, Uncle Joe is okay, both your cousins were away on business so they're okay, Lucy down the street's kids are okay…"

He called Valerie again. This time, she picked up—she had been stuck on a stalled train uptown when the first plane hit. One of their team members was on vacation and another had also been running late. They all checked in with each other, leaving robotic-sounding voicemails, as everyone struggled to make sense of what the hell happened.

He checked the rest of his voicemails. Dougie had called. He called him back and heard relief in his voice. They didn't talk long. What was there to say?

He stumbled down the hall to the bathroom, where he sank

to his knees in front of the toilet and vomited. His breath came in shuddering gasps as he emptied his stomach of last night's dinner. He got up, rinsed his mouth with a swig of electric blue mouthwash. He returned to his bedroom and flopped down on the mattress, where he emitted huge, noiseless sobs that shook the bed. After his shudders subsided, he noticed his left hand was twitching. It was slow at first, almost imperceptible, but he could feel it. It became a steadier beat, matching the voicemail alert blinking on his phone. Another message awaited him. He couldn't take listening to another frantic voice right then, so he ignored it. He stared at his hand, counting the number of times it twitched as he nodded off to sleep.

The sun was setting when he woke up. He showered and dressed. He'd told Dougie earlier that he'd meet him at The Anchor for a drink, as if a single pint of beer could make up for any of today.

He walked the three blocks to the bar. He swung open the door and was surprised to find that all the lights were on in the normally dim space. The high-top tables had been pushed together and were covered in platters of sandwiches and deli meats. The bar staff and some regulars, including Dougie, formed an assembly line, making sandwich after sandwich.

Dougie greeted him with a half-hearted high five. "Hungry?"

"Who are these for?" He took a sip of the beer Dougie handed him.

"Firefighters and other first responders," someone said.

"Of course." He hadn't eaten all day. Could he grab one himself? He hated himself for even thinking that. He put the glass down and caught a packaged loaf of bread as it was tossed to him.

"Larry!" A female voice that he didn't recognize was calling to him from across the bar.

He and Dougie turned. It was Sarah Malone from college. Larry had taken some classes with her and had a few mutual acquaintances. She was a nice, cool girl to talk with on the walk to class or while waiting in line at the cafeteria.

He walked over to say hello.

"I called you." She put her hand over her mouth and burst into tears.

"You did?" He was confused. His after-college days were those of a shaky transition from analog to digital, when people relied on memory and palm-sized address books to stay in touch. How had his phone number scored a space in either of hers?

"I thought the worst." She let out a long, shaky breath, then smiled.

"Do you know anyone who, you know?" He handed her a napkin from the sandwich table.

"Nobody. Thank God." She dabbed at her eyes. "Amazing. You know how many people I know who work or live downtown?"

It hit him then that there would be former classmates who weren't coming home that night. His whole body shivered and his hand twitched. Sarah touched his arm. They locked eyes.

"Coming through." One of the staff members wheeled by a hand truck piled with cases of bottled water.

They walked back to the sandwich line. Dougie raised an eyebrow at him, but he ignored it and got back to work. They made dozens of sandwiches. Volunteers came to pick them up, and they made more. After about two hours, Larry, Sarah, and Dougie took a few sandwiches for themselves and wolfed them down in the corner, chewing in companionable silence. Either Larry was starving, or this was the most delicious ham and Swiss he had ever eaten.

After the last of the sandwiches were picked up, he walked Sarah home to her apartment a few blocks away. She was born in Brooklyn, but like him, she didn't want to move back home with her parents and so had taken advantage of cheaper rents in Staten Island. They agreed how cool it was to have found decent places within walking distance of the ferry. They admired the luxury condo complex—what would be their future home—that had broken ground that spring.

The NYC skyline smoldered in the distance.

She stood on the first step of the stoop leading to her small apartment building and looked into his eyes. She threw her arms around him, and they kissed. A deep, passionate kiss with a slight mustard aftertaste. When they came up for air, it was with no small amount of guilt on his part for feeling that good. He didn't know how to react, how to dial up or down his emotions on such a terrible, terrible day.

Before he got into bed around midnight, he noticed he had one unplayed voicemail on his phone. He punched a button and listened. It was Sarah's message from that morning. The concern in her voice touched him. This was a person who cared about other people. He played it again several times, putting his phone on the pillow next to his head. It sounded like she was there next to him.

They had made a date for dinner that following Saturday. Afterward, they strolled along the promenade in St. George, staring out at the huge gap in the skyline. They held hands. It felt right, like a key fitting into a lock. When they kissed again, it was even better than their first kiss. Now there was hope. Permission had been granted. The universe had looked down on them and said, "Go ahead, you two. Something nice has to come out of this horrible mess."

He put off making love to her as long as he could stand it, which is to say their fourth date. He wanted her to think he was a gentleman, or at least trying very hard to be one. But when she pushed him onto her bed and perched herself on top of him, he knew she no longer cared about polite restraint. As their mouths found each other's in the dark, she let out a contented sigh. It told him all he needed to know: This was right, this was good, and this could mean forever, if they wanted it to.

Chapter 8

L arry had to get to the garbage before Sarah got rid of it.

He raced home, dropped his bag, threw his coat and hat over a dining room chair, and ran into the kitchen. He flung open the cabinet underneath the kitchen sink.

The overflowing garbage pail reeked, but it was perfume to his nose. A collage of limp banana peels mingled with coffee grounds. The soggy remains of beef stew splashed across a canvas of crushed lavender cupcakes.

He rolled up his sleeves and was ready to dive into that glorious mess when he saw a pair of rubber gloves shoved behind a can of oven cleaner. They were Barbie pink nightmares "manicured" with long red ovals at each tip—a gag gift from Sarah's bridal shower.

He stretched one glove over each hand, grimacing as the rubber pulled at the hair on his forearms. Swathed halfway up to his elbows, he began digging.

A few seconds later, Sarah walked in.

"What are you doing?" She sounded more grossed out than

she was suspicious. Her nose twitched at the stink.

He waved a rubber hand at her, as if he were Miss America. He had a prepared excuse. "I threw away a coupon this morning by mistake." It wasn't a lie; he had indeed thrown away a small pile of coupons from the local business circular that came in the mail.

He held one up for her to see.

"Pet food?"

"I'm sure someone we know can use it."

Sarah shook her head. She was wearing a blazer and a silk blouse over dark jeans and tall boots.

"You look nice. New client?"

"Hope so. Big one, too." She bounced on toes and wiggled her fingers at her side like she always did when she was excited. It reminded him of a gymnast about to start a floor routine. But the last time she had attempted a cartwheel, she knocked all the pictures off the wall in the hallway. They had both collapsed in laughter, then rehung the frames together.

"Nice. Good luck."

She smiled. Then she raised an eyebrow at him before leaving him with his mess.

He waited for the front door to slam shut before he went back to it. He tossed the pet food coupon back where it belonged and dug deeper, the smooshed lavender cupcakes mocking him.

And there it was. Such a small, inconsequential slip of paper. Crumpled a bit, but otherwise intact. He wiped a smudge of lavender icing off the corner of the lottery ticket, then put it on the floor, far away from any garbage. He threw all the trash back in the bag, tied it up, and tossed it aside.

He peeled off the gloves and washed his hands. Once, twice, three times. It appeared that his old habit of washing hands like he was prepping for surgery had returned. He would worry about that another time.

Hands spotless, he picked the ticket up.

He cradled it in the palm of his hand.

Could it be?

Nah.

Holding the ticket up like a waiter carrying a platter, he walked over to his work bag. He grabbed the newspaper and threw it onto the countertop. Still with his hand aloft, he flipped through until he found the page with the numbers. He placed the ticket next to the newspaper and took a deep breath.

Then he read each number out loud, his head swiveling back and forth—newspaper, ticket, newspaper, ticket.

1.

There was a 1.

8.

There was an 8.

11.

There was an 11.

And so on. Each one of the seven numbers matched. So did that last damn bonus number. Freaking 27.

"Jesus H. Christ."

He held the ticket up to the light, looking at the numbers from a different angle.

He banged his palms three times on the countertop.

Wait. What if there were a typo in the numbers in the newspaper? He reached for his phone, pulled up the web browser, and typed in the lottery's website to double check the winning numbers.

They all matched.

His hand twitched three times, sending his phone sailing through the air. It landed face down with a crack on the part of the tile floor that was mortgaged. But not for much longer. And he could buy any phone he darn well pleased now.

He looked again at the numbers in the newspaper, then back at the ones on the ticket.

He checked the date.

There was no mistake.

He won.

"Fuck you, Gaurav." He yelled it and he didn't care who heard.

The number twenty-seven exploded in his mind.

He saw zeros. Lots of them.

He had always liked being an accountant. But now, here he was on his hands and knees, thanking God and every living creature on the face of the earth, that he had chosen the best possible profession for himself.

Despite his naïveté regarding the actual Power Payday game, he had read in the news over the years the cautionary tales of past winners from all over the country. Although the details varied, there was one overriding theme: None of these people had any clue what to do when they had that many zeros added to their bank accounts overnight.

Nope. Not him. This would be his finest hour. He was going to avoid all the hijinks and hoopla that came with winning the lottery. He would live the rest of his life as a gazillionaire. He would not be the subject of some pathetic story in any newspaper. Not that he wanted to be the subject of a happy story, either. He was sick to his stomach when he thought of the press conference he would have to endure as a lottery winner. He would be forced to smile and shake hands with a person from the New York State Gaming Commission, who would hand him one of those huge checks printed on card stock so that the amount of the jackpot would show up in the photo. That photo would then be sent to every newspaper in each of the states where Power Payday was played. That had been another horrendous revelation to him— the bigger lottery games were part of a national network. Made in the Shade was exclusive to New York State. Power Payday, on the other hand, was offered in forty states and a few U.S. territories. It was unnerving that people in Guam might come to know the name Larry Sortino.

The only way he could avoid all that was to keep his identity under wraps.

The first idea that popped into his head was that he would

claim the ticket anonymously. But a quick scan of the rules and regulations on the New York Lottery website—now there was some fine print for you—told him that he was out of luck. He would have to identify himself as the bearer of the winning ticket to claim the prize.

He clenched his jaw. Hard. Sweat formed on his upper lip. He imagined his brain to be like the inner workings of a watch, the tiny teeth of the cogs and wheels tick tocking away as he tried to find a way out of this terrible, yet wonderful situation.

He stepped out onto his terrace and stared out at the neighboring building with the unused and unloved balconies. He'd made assumptions about his rich neighbors, how they took their real estate for granted. But what did he know about any of them? Or what it was like to be rich, for that matter? Maybe they were wealthy invalids, though if they were, wouldn't fresh air be a good thing? Maybe the paparazzi hounded his reality television star neighbor. What if it wasn't just the paparazzi who spied on rich people? What if the nonprofits had their own band of spies who camped out beneath the terraces of luxury apartment buildings? *Look, 5B bought a new set of patio furniture! They have money to burn! Send them our new fundraising brochure!*

He peered over the side of his terrace and swept his eyes over the sidewalk that stretched the length of the building. No one in sight.

Then he remembered camera drones. They were the new way for tabloids to keep up with celebrities. No one could escape a drone. In recent news, a member of the British royal family had knocked one out of the air with a well-aimed croquet mallet, and the newspaper had had the gall to sue for damages.

His hands turned clammy, his mouth dry like sand.

He tripped over the threshold of the French door as he went back inside. He locked it and jiggled the handle three times. He went into the kitchen and gulped down a glass of water.

He was in trouble. If he couldn't claim this thing without

anyone knowing, he would need a foolproof plan to keep him and his money safe.

Or rather, his and Sarah's money.

He'd almost forgotten about her. His body grew cold. Would money keep them together? Would they be like that couple on her favorite reality TV show who hated each other but loved their joint bank account? And what about all those horrendous relatives who crawled out from wherever they had been hiding to ask for money?

Fortunately, his and Sarah's families were small. They would both want to make sure everyone was taken care of, but there weren't many people on either side of the family tree to worry about. She was also an only child. Her parents lived quite happily in a small condo on the beach in Hilton Head half the year and spent the other half on cruise ships. On his side, there was his Uncle Joe in Boca Raton, his mother's younger brother. He would have to call him and break the news gently because the man just had a brand-new pacemaker installed. Uncle Joe's kids, Rob and Amy, his older cousins, had settled down somewhere in South Jersey, but he only saw them once every couple of years. That was the extent of his family.

As for charities, of course he would donate. He wasn't that much of a tightwad. He was happy to have already given a little money to some of the more popular organizations. He always gave a few bucks to the cancer foundation that sent him the free address labels. He couldn't resist giving some money to the children's foundation that encouraged him to send back the enclosed birthday card to a child undergoing treatment at the hospital. And though he never had a pet in his life, those TV commercials with the dogs shivering in the snow set against the music of that singer Sarah loved so much made him reach for his checkbook. He was always a sucker for a good commercial. But even though he had money now (okay, a shit ton of it, to be more exact), he also didn't feel the need to bankroll all the charities in the Tri-State area.

He sat down on the couch, but he slid right off because of the wall of throw pillows Sarah had arranged there. With a swipe of his arm, he sent them tumbling to the floor.

He stared out the window past the neighboring building to the New York skyline.

The skyline stared at him.

He blinked.

The lights of the Freedom Tower blinked back.

He was in a vulnerable position. He recalled from the lottery website that when a winning combination was discovered, the New York State Gaming Commission could track the ticket back to the store of purchase. He envisioned the Bay Street Mini Mart as a flashing red dot on the map on a computer screen at the Gaming Commission's headquarters, which in his head resembled a mission control center like the one at NASA.

"There it is!" someone would shout, and a crew of serious-looking men and women would trot over to stare at an infrared map on a screen.

In his mind's eye, he saw the flashing red dot on the map, the Bay Street Mini Mart. Then he saw another dot *bloop* up onto the screen—his condo. Two places so close together on the map, as if they were one and the same.

He, like his phone, was toast.

His hand twitched. Would they do a door-to-door search of his building, like the prize patrol on those magazine sweepstakes commercials? Did the New York State Gaming Commission employ people to do that? He saw them, a team of smiling men and women walking in lockstep, carrying that absurdly large check for the photo op. They were coming for him. Coming to change his life.

"Stop it!" The words came out in a whimper.

He was exposed. He needed to hide. But why? He wasn't a fugitive.

He ducked and rolled onto the floor, landing on top of the pillows. Sarah was right. They were very soft. He arranged one under his head, one under his knees, and a third under his ankles. He breathed in until he felt his lungs would explode, then slowly let it out with a whistle. He reached for the fuzzy orange blanket draped along an arm of the couch, also a new purchase made during her latest shopping spree. It looked horrendous, but it was warm. He pulled the blanket over himself, though he knew it would be impossible to be seen from the window at this angle.

He was cozy, cuddled up as he was in the orange nightmare. He could fall asleep right there. But he couldn't risk Sarah coming home to find him on the floor like this.

He tossed off the blanket and stretched his body. He pumped his arms and legs as if he were making a snow angel in the carpet. The movement was good. It allowed him to relax for a moment, to breathe without gasping. But he panicked all over again when he remembered the ticket. That fragile, minuscule piece of paper worth so much damn money. What was he supposed to do with the actual ticket?

He read the instructions again. They were clear: Sign it and turn it into the Gaming Commission to claim the prize. There were over a dozen claim centers in the state and also a mailing address in Schenectady where he could send his ticket. He cackled. As if he would ever stick this treasure in an envelope and put a stamp on it! He would not let it leave his sight. Scratch that—he wouldn't let it leave his person.

For a long moment, he gave serious consideration to the idea of sewing it to himself. But he knew that would be painful. He had a better idea. He started to get up, but he saw the bright lights of the city out the window and dove back onto the floor. He crawled over to his work bag and dug through it until he found the lanyard from which had hung his Parker & Rosenthal ID. On his last day, he had to leave his ID, but he'd kept the lanyard and the attached clear plastic case. He wasn't sure why he brought it with him. He hated that lanyard. It was downright dangerous. He'd got it caught in doors at the office all the time. Once, it wrapped around a handle and the door slammed shut behind him. His ID was on one side of the locked door, and he was tethered on the other side by his lanyard. He had to bend down so the damn thing didn't asphyxiate him. It was a good thing the door was glass. A coworker saw his arms flailing and ran over to save him.

He slid the ticket into the case. It fit. Plenty of room to spare. He turned the case upside down and shook it. Too much room. The ticket slid right out. *Shit.* He eyed the stapler on his desk and crawled over to get it. He swung an arm up and brought the stapler down in one smooth motion. He stapled the top of the pouch three times. He turned the pouch over and shook it again. The ticket slid, then stopped where the three staples sealed off the opening. He bit his lip. Not good enough. With the precision of a surgeon, he clicked a neat line of silver metal around the ticket. He made a full border before he ran out of staples.

He shook the pouch. The ticket didn't move.

He smiled.

Now for the lanyard.

Last year when they reissued staff IDs to all the employees, the company saved thousands of dollars by forgoing the premium lanyards printed with the Parker & Rosenthal logo, opting instead for the cheap, no-frills kind. He held the nylon lanyard in his hand. It looked like a long red shoelace, with the aglets poking through the two holes in the plastic case. He tied double knots at the end of the string, pulling and tugging to make sure they stayed put. He placed the lanyard around his neck, so the ticket hung down to the middle of his chest. It reminded him of that rapper from way back who wore a clock on a thick chain around his neck. He stuck it inside his shirt and flattened it out. He buttoned his collar around the lanyard and was pleased to see that it was hidden. He was glad it was winter. He could always wear a scarf as an added layer of protection.

He marine crawled over to the full-length mirror on the wall inside the bedroom. He pulled himself up onto his knees to admire his new look. The lanyard was secure, invisible. He could feel the plastic-encased ticket warm against his chest. He moved his neck into various positions. He looked like the world's worst dancer attempting an old-school pop and lock move. Never mind. It worked. He couldn't see the lanyard or the ticket from any angle.

Excellent. This was a strong start to his plan. This was how he would protect his prize until he could figure out what the hell to do next.

He got up from his knees and stared at himself in the mirror.

He breathed in, puffing out his chest until he felt he might burst. He pounded a fist against his chest where the ticket hung. He pounded the other fist. Then again. He looked like an out-of-shape Tarzan.

Then he hollered. And the sound echoed across his kingdom.

Part 2

February

Chapter 9

L arry Sortino, lottery winner.

Larry Sortino, gazillionaire.

Larry Sortino, king of his kingdom, at last.

Well, not yet. But soon.

Maybe.

He needed time to absorb it all. As an accountant, he understood money more than most, but up until now, it had always been other people's money. Back at Parker & Rosenthal, he would marvel at how hard some of his clients worked to build their businesses before they turned a profit. All he had to do was make some good guesses that took about three minutes. That meant he earned about 191 million dollars per minute.

It didn't seem fair.

Then, there was the Island Tax Prep issue. He couldn't quit a job he just started. Besides, it was tax season, his favorite time of year.

He continued to have his morning coffee on the terrace. He showered, got dressed, and took the short walk to work, looking over his shoulder every so often to make sure no one saw him. As far as the rest of the world knew—well, at least Sarah, Dougie, and a few assorted neighbors who might know his daily routine— he was still commuting to Manhattan five times a week.

He'd stopped by the Bay Street Mini Mart once since that night, but it was to fill up his car, not go inside. A huge banner hung from the store's awning: LOTTERY JACKPOT WON HERE!!! He found the three exclamation points unnecessary and a bit vulgar.

What if he'd walked into the store and the ticket around his neck set off an alarm, like that time he was in a department store with Sarah and she walked too close to the entrance with a vase in her hands? He was certain the little slip of paper he wore like jewelry didn't have that kind of high-tech capability, but he hadn't wanted to chance it. Although he did wonder if Sunil continued to put his scratch-off cards aside for him each week.

With tax season underway, the office hummed. A steady flow of clients came through the door each day. When they left, they all had a similar look of triumph on their faces, an expression that said, "Thank goodness that's done."

He didn't have as much time in between clients for the crossword anymore, so he talked to Jordan whenever there was downtime. Or rather, Jordan talked, and he listened. Jordan had an opinion on just about everything, from sports to politics to household appliances.

He had been wearing the lanyard for about two weeks when he asked Jordan for his insight on the lottery.

"Why do you torment me?" Jordan said. He stomped off to the backroom for a second doughnut from the two dozen Larry had splurged on for his coworkers that morning. Jordan was likeable, but the knucklehead had a flair for the dramatic that tended to grate on the rest of the staff. The recent change of events had increased Larry's patience, though. Perhaps this could be his new hobby. St. Larry, Patron Saint of Put-Upon Coworkers.

"Seriously, dude, you've been here for, like, two weeks." Jordan had been trying to give up his e-cigarette habit, but it didn't seem to be going well.

"I come in peace." Larry raised his hands in mock surrender.

Jordan rolled his chair to the other side of Larry's desk. "Fine. Ask me again."

Larry put his palms on the desk and leaned forward. "If you had won that huge lottery jackpot, what would you have done?"

Jordan closed his eyes and took in a deep breath. He couldn't help but be pleased that his question garnered such serious thought, even though he wasn't so sure Jordan was capable of much serious thought.

"I would have passed out." He brushed powdered sugar off his shirt. "Then, when I came to, I'd have gone out to celebrate. Later, I'd have passed out again, but this time from drinking." Jordan looked pleased with his answer.

"No, I mean, what would you do about the money?"

"Oh. Gotcha."

Jordan closed his eyes again and took another deep breath. Larry braced himself.

"First, I'd say 'Fuck you' to every person who had wronged me." Jordan whispered the "Fuck you" part. There were clients in the office. "Then, I'd go buy a new car." He chewed his lip with defiance.

The speed of his answer proved that yes, this was indeed a question Jordan had pondered before.

"No, that's not what I mean, either. Before all that." Again, he felt a surge of patience as if he had all the time in the world. It was like that time last summer when he taught the young kid down the hall how to tie his shoes. By the time the kid had mastered it, a half-hour had passed like it was nothing. "How would you claim the money?" He tried to sound casual, just shooting the breeze.

Jordan slapped his forehead with his palm. "Oh. My bad." He seemed disappointed that this is what Larry was getting at. But he had an answer. "You do what it says on the back of the ticket. Sign it, mail it into the Gaming Commission." He scrunched up his mouth. "But let's be real, who would do that? Trust your winning ticket to the United States Postal Service? Nah, I'd take it straight to a lottery service center."

Larry stared at Jordan. This was a guy who could read and comprehend the fine print, at least when it meant something good was in it for him. But then desperation started to return.

"There's no other way?" He felt hot. He took off his jacket and started to loosen his tie. "No less conspicuous way to claim the prize?" He touched his chest, felt the edges of the plastic holder through his shirt and undershirt. He pretended he had an itch, but Jordan didn't seem to notice he was scratching his chest like he had just belly flopped in some poison ivy.

"Why would you want to hide it?" Jordan's tone was incredulous, perhaps even a bit insulted. "Isn't winning the lottery every human's dream? You hit the big jackpot, you hire a car to take you to claim the check—take the lump sum, don't be stupid—and then it's press conference, press conference, press conference." He got up and strutted down the aisle between desks like a runway model.

Jordan might have been disgruntled at first by hypothetical talk about winning the lottery, but now he was enjoying himself. Irving and some of the others had come over to witness the spectacle, even Jeanette, who preferred to knit between client appointments and never seemed to leave her desk. She brought her needles, yarn, and what looked like a sock. Yes, it was a sock. Either Jeanette had gotten better at knitting, or Larry was better at identifying what she was knitting.

"Ten o'clock news. Eleven o'clock news. Front page of all the newspapers. The actual front page, not just the homepage on the website. You're not in the news, you are the news." Jordan ended his strut and jiggled his hips. Everyone laughed. He bowed.

"Right, but then you run like hell," Irving said.

"Man, you had to burst my bubble." Jordan snapped back upright. "Wrong week to give up the e-cig." He looked around to make sure no clients were nearby, then he pulled a small metal device out of his inner jacket pocket. He took a puff, then exhaled a cloud of vapor.

Jeanette shook her head in disapproval.

Larry turned to look at Irving. "Run from what?"

"Jordan, you really need to give that up," Irving said.

"Run from what, Irving?"

"I know, Irv, I know. Baby steps," Jordan said.

"They say e-cigarettes can be even worse than regular—"

"RUN FROM WHAT?"

All eyes turned to Larry. Yup, that had come out as a shout. The lanyard hidden under his shirt sliced into his skin. The metal clip had caught on a hair and yanked it out of his chest. It was all he could do to keep from howling like a werewolf in transition. Is that what waxing felt like? People paid for that agony in the name of self-care?

"Everyone," said Irving, who seemed to take his outburst in stride. "Everything. Schools. Charities. Money-hungry relatives coming out of the woodwork. Everyone wants a piece of you."

"Especially in New York. The absolute worst lottery stories come out of New York." Jordan looked pleased with his knowledge of this bit of trivia.

Irving nodded so hard it looked like his head was about to pop off his neck. "Remember that family upstate? They got roped into donating money to a charity that didn't even exist."

"That's nothing. What about that family in Westchester who kept having 'cousins' show up on their doorstep?" Jordan made quotation marks with the index and middle fingers of both hands, clawing at the air. "That's what happens when you win the lottery and your last name is Smith."

Everyone laughed except Larry. He was too busy reminding himself to breathe in through his nose, out through his mouth.

Jordan and Irving continued sharing other cautionary lottery tales.

"How 'bout that married couple?" A wicked smile spread across Irving's face. "The ones who were so happy and in love before the money, but then the wife demanded her half and ran off with her husband's best friend?"

The little gurgling noise that came out of Larry's throat, which felt like a boa constrictor was tightening around it, was drowned out by everyone's laughter.

This was agony. He had figured going to work and keeping up with his normal routine was a good idea, but now he saw he'd been dead wrong. If his coworkers would shut up for a single moment, they'd notice he had turned gray and was clutching his chest. They might ask him if he was having a heart attack. They didn't. Fine, maybe he wasn't having a heart attack, but he wasn't okay.

He mouthed, "Excuse me" and darted off to the bathroom. He made it in time to puke up his breakfast. Thank God for that noisy exhaust fan. Although at the rate his loquacious coworkers were going, they wouldn't have heard a single retch.

He stood over the sink and stared at the water as it flowed from the tap. He willed himself to wash his hands once and only once. Success. He splashed water on his face and dried his hands by running them through his hair, which he allowed himself to do three times.

He looked in the mirror. He almost didn't recognize the frightened man who stared back. "What happened to you?" His voice was hoarse.

He flushed the toilet, washed his hands again, and went back to his desk. Everyone was still crowded around, laughing at yet another of Irving's stories.

"Penniless?" Jordan asked.

"Pen-ni-less," Irving said.

The group cackled.

"What would you do, Larry?" Irving asked.

"With what?"

"With the money?"

The lanyard was tight around his neck. His mouth was bone dry. He went to the water cooler and filled up a small cup with ice cold water. He wanted to throw it in his own face but settled for drinking it down. He wished it were a shot of vodka or tequila instead.

"I would pay off my mortgage."

Jordan yelled, "Boring!" and they all collapsed into laughter again.

He waved. "Hi. I'm Larry Sortino, and I'm a boring person."

Jeanette had stopped knitting and scratched her head with a knitting needle. "I think they mean, like, where would you go shopping, Larry."

He started to answer, but his mouth hung open. Nothing. He had no idea.

Here he was, sitting on five hundred seventy-five million dollars, and he didn't know how he was going to spend a single penny of it. Paying off his mortgage was the small dream of a small man. There was so much more for him now, wasn't there? Still, he had no clue what to do with any of it.

Why couldn't he have had a pat answer like Jordan? He was right. Many people dreamt of winning the lottery and knew how they would spring into action if money ever were to miraculously show up in their lives. It had been a hypothetical question, of course, but coming up with any real answer to it made him dizzy. Still, his coworkers wanted one. They all looked at him and waited. It got awkward.

Jordan feigned falling asleep and let out a loud snore.

"Oh, who knows." He forced himself to sound cheery and breezy. "Knowing me, I'd probably go food shopping without coupons."

"I'm not surprised." Irving slapped him on the back.

"That's so you." Jordan offered him a fist bump.

"You know me." He returned it.

Or did they? He wasn't even sure he knew himself anymore.

Chapter 10

There was one thing Larry did know—he would have to tell Sarah. As his wife, she was entitled to half of his payout. He didn't begrudge her any of it, not even after her shenanigans with Dougie. After all, there was just so much of it. What would happen when he told her? Would she stay with him, or would she take her half and leave?

Whenever he had imagined paying off their mortgage, whenever he dreamed of winning enough money at scratch-offs to travel again, he always assumed Sarah would be part of it all. Of course, the money he'd been aiming for was always manageable. The goal was security.

But this was five hundred seventy-five million dollars.

He wrote some figures down on a sheet of paper. His head spun. He grabbed his calculator, but the screen wasn't big enough for his calculations. It came up with an E for error whenever he tried to multiply something.

It was too much money. What had he done to earn it? Nothing. His rich clients all had stories behind their money.

The companies they built. The real estate they bought and sold. Even that third-generation heiress who didn't do much of anything was able to point to whatever it was the previous two generations of her family did to earn it and say, "There. That's where my money came from."

What would his mother have said about all of this? He remembered the pride on her face when she got the keys to her first lavender car. He knew how hard she had worked for it. It was a prize well deserved. A lump grew in his throat. His prize came from the minimal energy it took to make eight random guesses and fill in some numbered circles with a golf pencil. Pathetic. Unearned. Undeserved.

He continued to set an early alarm every night. He'd get up the next morning, drink his coffee on the terrace, and go to work. Rinse and repeat. It was all he could think to do right now. He was thankful for the distractions Island Tax Prep afforded him, even though he felt bad about keeping a job that someone else needed way more than he did.

There was plenty to keep him busy, and there was also enough to keep him amused. It was an understatement to say that there were some oddball characters on Staten Island. Now with tax season well underway, many of them came in the door of Island Tax Prep.

There was the frat boy from St. John's who worked the front desk at the campus gym.

"Don't forget, dude. I donated twelve dollars to my fraternity's charity," the boy said.

Larry noted his donation.

"Hey, how much is Uncle Sammy going to give me for spring break in Cancun?" Frat Boy stared at him with the expectancy of a child on Christmas Eve.

"Let me see." He punched a couple of keys on the computer. "It looks like you'll get about two hundred back."

"Woo hoo!" Frat Boy ran to the window and waved at the car that waited outside. Assorted arms, hands, and even a bare foot (in this weather?) stuck out of the windows to wave back at him.

"Man, you are awesome." Frat Boy settled back into the chair opposite Larry's desk. "I'm gonna send the rest of my bros to see you. Well, the ones who have jobs, anyway."

And so it went.

There was the retired accountant. He smiled at Larry. "Are you a CPA?"

"I am."

"So am I."

"Then why am I doing your taxes?"

"I'm retired. Can't be bothered. Besides, I hate it when numbers get personal."

Larry admired how the man could detach himself from his money like that.

Of course, he got his share of anxious customers too. Those people who still brought in receipts in a shoe box and wrung their hands while they watched him figure it all out.

"Will I be audited?" asked an English teacher at an all-girls' Catholic school. She'd bought a ton of school supplies and was hoping to write them off on her taxes.

"Well, have you withheld any other income paperwork from me?"

"No. What you have there, that's all I received from my employer."

"Then you should be fine."

Ms. English Teacher looked over the desk full of papers. He gave her a reassuring smile. She gnawed at a thumbnail.

As tax season ramped up, Larry was busy with an appointment every hour or so. He returned to his *Times* crossword if he had a bit of time in between appointments, but gone were the days when he had the time to finish it.

When Jordan had downtime, he practiced his perfect news desk posture and murmured phrases he had scribbled on index cards.

"Round and round the ragged rock the ragged rascal ran,"

Jordan recited over and over again. He repeated them using different intonations, sometimes rolling his Rs like an Italian opera singer. He said the words in a high-pitched voice, then in a very low voice. Larry hoped Jordan would practice his words using an accent, like an Irish brogue or something. That would be fun. But Jordan was working hard to get rid of his New Yawk accent to begin with, so picking up another wouldn't have been in his best interest.

He knew the other staff members were annoyed by Jordan's antics, but he didn't mind. They reminded him of his time at Wagner College, when he would walk past the theater at night and hear the student performers at rehearsal, the sounds of their vocal exercises floating through the open windows. It soothed him to know that people cared so much about doing something well that they warmed up for the effort. All he had was his stupid calculator.

One afternoon, Larry joined Irving in the break room to get a cup of coffee.

"How's it going?" Irving asked.

"Not bad. You've got some characters that come in here."

They both took a sip of the bitter coffee and listened to Jordan, who had moved on to a different index card with new phrases.

"Red leather, yellow leather. Red leather, yellow leather."

He cocked his head at Jordan and grinned at Irving. "Got some characters who work here, too."

Irving laughed as they walked back to the main office. "We had an employee who did taxes for us in between auditions in the city. Said he liked it here because the clients inspired his craft."

"Inspiring is one word for it. You know, it's funny. My condo isn't too far from here. I can't believe I haven't seen anyone in here I know yet."

Just then, the front door opened and the bell tinkled.

"Larry Sortino."

He knew that voice.

He touched his chest, where the ticket was.

Everybody looked up. His hand twitched once, then again.

It was Monica Rossi, in the flesh.

Monica Rossi of the society column.

Monica Scotto of his college days.

Monica, the girl that got away.

Well, sort of.

"It *is* you," she said.

How her blue eyes sparkled.

Jordan gave up on his index cards and gaped at Larry.

In fact, everyone in the office, including the clients, had paused and stared at him, slack-jawed.

He walked over and greeted her with a hug. "Hi, stranger."

He was enveloped in a scent that he couldn't name, but she smelled like this candle Sarah had bought once and never used. It was so expensive she couldn't even bring herself to light the wick.

Monica stood eye to eye with him. He remembered being a whole head taller than her in college. He glanced down to hold back the fierce blush he knew was coming and saw that she was wearing four-inch heels.

He looked around at his coworkers, who all snapped back to whatever they had been doing.

Jordan opened his textbook and started highlighting with a fury.

Jeanette's knitting needles were a blur.

"I'm going to refill the water cooler," Irving announced. This was a big deal. Last time, he'd dropped the jug and caused a flash flood.

Larry gestured to his desk. "Come have a seat."

He wondered who did Monica's taxes. He bet her accountant had a much nicer office, or at least more to offer than a folding chair and a plastic cup of water.

They sat down. "It's good to see you," he said.

"You too. I was passing by and happened to look in the window. I couldn't believe it was you." She clapped her hands together and her bracelets jingled.

He shrugged his shoulders and smiled. "It's me." He wished they were anywhere but inside Island Tax Prep.

"How long have you been working here? I thought you were a CPA at some firm in the city?"

Interesting. Maybe she had been keeping tabs on him all along, too?

"Yes, for fifteen years at Parker and Rosenthal. Been there since we graduated." Larry gathered a few papers and tapped the edge of the stack on his desk. He hoped it made him look like he was important. "Trying something new. I might take the plunge some day and open my own firm, so I figured I'd get to know my neighbors a little better first."

She cocked her head to one side. "Oh, Larry. You got laid off?"

He slapped the desk three times with his hand. She jumped. He needed to change the subject.

"I saw your picture in the paper."

"Which one?"

"Which paper?"

"No, I mean, which picture?"

"Oh. Right. So many. You're all over. Kind of hard to miss." She smiled.

"Um, I think it was for the Saturn Ball at the museum."

"Jupiter Ball."

"Jupiter Ball. Right. You were with Max, of course. He looks good. Very, um, photogenic."

"Yes. Sammy takes after him." She reached into her purse for her phone, swiped at the screen with a manicured index finger, then showed the phone to him. Her home screen had a picture of a young child. He stared for a moment. Of course she had a child. Why wouldn't she? It's what people did. They got married and had children.

"He looks like you." His voice didn't sound like his own.

"What about you? Married? House? Kids?"

"Well, we..."

A crash sounded from the coffee break area, followed by a muffled expletive. Then an audible rush of water. Not good.

The doorbell tinkled and, as if on cue, the water cooler man entered with a delivery.

Monica stood up. "I should go. You have a customer."

"It's the water delivery man." Larry waved to the guy.

"But you're at work. I'm intruding."

He smiled. She smiled back. Or at least it looked like she was trying to smile. Maybe she was in pain? Her features were frozen, as if she couldn't open her mouth all the way.

"I'm very happy to see you, Larry." But she looked anything but happy.

"Are you okay?"

"I'm sorry. It's the fillers. Just had them done. This is about all the emotion I'm allowed right now. Try me again in thirty-six to forty-eight hours."

He followed her to the door. He bent toward her, and they kissed each other on the cheek. Hers felt like a block of ice. He wondered if she even felt the kiss.

She threw her arms around his neck and hugged him tight. "Take care."

"You too."

And then she was gone.

He rubbed the back of his neck, tapped it three times, and turned back toward his desk.

Everyone, including the water delivery guy, was staring at him.

Jordan popped into view, and Irving, mop in hand, stretched around the corner to look at him too.

"Hey now. What was that all about?" Jordan snapped his fingers and wiggled his hips. Larry couldn't help but laugh.

Irving looked at the puddle of water sloshing around his

feet. "Yeah, spill it. Heh, funny."

Jordan launched into investigative reporter mode. He grabbed his highlighter like a microphone. "Larry Sortino. How in the world are you so chummy with Mrs. Country Club-slash-Charity Ball Queen?" He thrust the highlighter into Larry's face for a response.

"Huh?"

Irving shook his head in wonder. "I didn't think she was three-dimensional."

Jordan kept up with his line of questioning. "And she stopped by to say hello to *you*? Why? How do you know each other? When was the last time you saw each other? Will she be back to do her taxes?"

Larry gritted his teeth. An image of Monica on the first day of Financial Accounting flashed across his brain. That flick of her hair that undid him every time. His jaw relaxed as he remembered those days in college.

Yes, they had dated. They'd gone out on actual dates. To the movies. A round or two of miniature golf. Late night meals, nothing fancy, maybe a cheeseburger at the diner or tacos at that little Mexican spot not far from campus. They went to see shows at Irving Plaza and Roseland. He would stand behind her in the crowd and she would lean back into him, his hands on her hips. When he dropped her off at home after a night out together, they would make out and fog up the windows of his compact car.

Back on campus, it was a different story. An outsider would look at them and recognize a friendship, a good friendship, but nothing more. There was no holding hands, no touching each other at all. He told himself he wanted to be respectful, take things slow. But it got to a point where he couldn't concentrate on their conversations anymore, couldn't stay focused on what she was saying. He wanted her. She knew it.

One night, after eating slices of lemon meringue pie at the diner, Larry drove her home. They had been seeing each other for about two months. He turned his car down the long driveway of her parents' house, not far from school. The house was large enough to make him wonder if it could be classified as a mansion. He'd learned about different types of properties in his taxation class. It occurred to him that Monica never talked about what her parents did for a living. In fact, she hadn't talked about her parents much at all.

He parked the car, turned off the ignition, and reached for her.

She stopped him.

"What's the matter?" He looked in her eyes.

"Nothing. I want you to come in."

He shot out of the car and made it around to her side before she even opened her door. She laughed, then took his hand and led him to the front steps of the house.

It was happening. The massive stone steps of the home made him nervous. He stared up at the brick facade as his heart performed a drum solo in his chest.

Inside the house, which he decided could most certainly be classified as a mansion, the foyer was dark. It seemed like no one was home, but who could tell for sure?

"Parents home?"

"They're at a hospital benefit." Monica turned, pushed him up against the door, and kissed him hard. Her fingers danced along his belt buckle.

"Mon? That you, honey?" called a voice.

They sprang apart. A light came on.

Mrs. Scotto came into the hallway. She wore a beaded gown that dragged on the floor. One delicate high-heeled shoe was on her foot, and the other was in her hand. Her voice was steady, but her face betrayed the fact that she'd been crying. Dark circles ringed her eyes where her mascara and eyeliner smudged and ran together. She looked like Monica, but she was older, smaller, and so very sad.

"Ma, you're home already?"

His heart plummeted, but at the same time came an odd sense of relief.

"Yes. Home already." Mrs. Scotto held her hand out to him. "You must be Larry."

"Yes." He cleared his throat and moved forward a few steps to accept her handshake. "Larry Sortino. You look beautiful, Mrs. Scotto." And she was. A beautiful mess.

She smiled. "I did." She took off the other sandal and examined it.

Larry looked at Monica, whose face was taut with anger.

"Where's Dad?"

"Oh." Mrs. Scotto waved her hand through the air like she was swatting away a fly. She took off her other sandal. "He's still out. He had to attend to some...business." She hugged Monica and kissed her on the cheek. "Night, baby." She touched his shoulder. "S-so nice to meet you, Larry." It was then he heard the slur of her liquor-drenched words.

"Night." The way Monica said it, it sounded like a swear word.

Mrs. Scotto padded away barefoot, sandals in hand.

"I hate him."

Larry touched her shoulder and she flinched.

"I'm sorry," she said.

"There's nothing to—"

"You should go."

Damn it. Game over.

"Okay. I'll go."

He stood there. She stepped toward him and hugged him. She wrapped her arms around his waist and breathed in. "I'll see you Monday," she said.

It was May, and there was one more week left of their sophomore year. After exams were over, Monica packed to go to Italy with her mother. It was under the guise of some new business endeavor the Scottos were working on, but he surmised it had more to do with getting away from Mr. Scotto for a while.

He got a few postcards from her in the mail. They all said, "Love, Monica" on them, but he knew enough not to read anything into it.

Throughout the summer, he thought about that night at her house and what might have happened if not for the appearance of Mrs. Scotto. But he didn't worry too much. He was sure that he could have another chance with Monica when she returned from Italy right in time for the start of classes.

But Max Rossi transferred to Wagner for the start of their junior year, and that was the end of Larry and Monica.

It took Larry one look at Max to know that he did not like the guy. This was an unusual reaction for him. He prided himself on getting along with most people. He was a fan of humankind, one might say. He had an easy-going nature that made people like him back. That's how it had always been.

On the first day of the semester, Max sauntered into their Consumer Behavior class. Larry hadn't remembered this, but Sarah had been in that class, too, always slipping in the back at the last possible second. Her vantage point offered her a unique insight on Monica. "That girl had daddy issues," she said to him whenever she saw her picture in the paper. He had told his wife very little about his time with Monica. In the end, what was there to say?

He, on the other hand, had Max issues. He was repulsed by this slick dude who wore cologne like an extra sweater and slicked his hair back under a backwards Rangers cap, a stubborn curl peeking out through the opening. Maybe it was the Rangers cap. He hated it when teams from one sport put their logos on the uniforms of other sports. He didn't expect hockey fans to walk around wearing caged helmets, of course, but he did think it was dumb to have a baseball hat with a hockey team logo on it.

When Max sat down next to Monica, she smiled in a way that she had never smiled at Larry before. It was slow, as if her lips were undressing her teeth. Something hot and angry grew in his stomach. Max smiled back at Monica and tipped his damn hat at her.

Max, as everyone knew, was a member of the Rossi family. "You know, *those* Rossis," Dougie had once whispered to him, the way one always did when talking about one of the mafia families on Staten Island. But the Rossis didn't warrant a whisper, not anymore. The family had been involved with organized crime decades ago, but now, everyone knew that the family had downgraded their business deals from illegal to shady. You no longer went to them if you needed retaliation. But if you wanted in on a sports pool or wanted kitchen appliances at a good price, the Rossis were your people.

He hadn't cared about who Max's family was, or what they did or didn't do. What he did care about was that something had shifted in the classroom that day and tilted in the favor of two people, neither of whom were him.

"Earth to Larry." Irving made a motion with his hand to get on with it. Jordan hummed the theme song to *Jeopardy*.

Larry shrugged his shoulders. "We were friends in college. Well, more than friends, I guess. At one point. Maybe for a little while. Well, not really. But yes."

"Go on," Jordan said.

Irving grinned.

"But then Max Rossi transferred to Wagner, and that was the end of that."

"Damn," Jordan said.

"Left in the dust," Irving said.

Jordan gnawed at a hangnail. "You ever wonder if—"

"I try not to." His hand twitched three times. He hoped no one saw.

"Wait a minute," said Irving. "Aren't you married?"

"I am." He sounded like he was surprised. He hoped no one noticed that, too. But someone had.

"How's that going for you?" Jordan said.

Chapter 11

Larry heard voices as he opened the door to the condo. His shoulders slumped. So much for being alone with his thoughts for a while.

Sarah and Dougie were at the dining room table, playing cards. Both had ice packs on their necks, and both turned to him and winced in discomfort.

And then he saw the candlelit dinner for two set out on the table. "What's going on?"

"Hi hon, how was your day?"

Dougie saluted him with a hand wrapped in gauze, then went back to his cards.

Had she just called him "hon"? He was hit with a pang of hope, then confusion. Was he in the correct condo? He looked back at the front door. 5B. Yep, this was home all right.

"Fine. Yours?"

He looked at Dougie, who seemed a bit worse for wear, but not so injured as to prevent them from playing what looked like a game of Go Fish.

"Guys, what the hell is going on?"

"Dougie took me to get milk at the convenience store, and he lost control of the car," said Sarah.

"I told you it was black ice," said Dougie. "Go fish."

"He hit a nun and a priest."

"Their car. We hit their car."

Sarah put down her cards and smiled at Larry. "But Dougie and I are fine. So are Father Eric and Sister Josephine."

He didn't know what to do, so he sat down at the table.

They dealt him in. He picked up his cards. Why not? He had always liked Go Fish, come to think of it.

"Okay, anything else I should know about?" He was not in the mood to deal with this right now. Was there ever a good time for this sort of thing?

"Sarah and I have been screwing around behind your back for about five months." Dougie flicked his gaze to Sarah. "Right? About five months?"

She nodded.

Larry's foot twitched three times, but he managed to keep his voice calm.

"Five months behind my back? And how long right under my nose?"

Dougie's face took on a pained look. "You knew?"

Sarah sighed. "Oh, Larry. I knew you knew."

"Wait, you knew he did? He knew you did?" Dougie whipped his head back and forth between the two of them.

Larry asked Sarah for a six. She didn't have one, so he took a card from the pile.

"It's not rocket science, Douglas," he said.

Sarah asked for a five. Dougie handed her a five of clubs.

"You never said a word." She dropped the pair of fives on the table.

"You seemed happy." Larry rearranged his cards so they were in number order. At some point, he thought he would wake up from this crazy dream. But he could feel the cards in his hands. This was all happening.

"See? You were happy. Lah, got a seven?" Dougie's smug smile made him recoil.

"No. Go fish. Well, you were happy, and then you weren't, right, Sarah?"

The satisfied look slid off Dougie's face. One point for Team Larry.

Sarah's eyes filled with tears. "You're right. I was, then I wasn't."

As if they were doing a staged reading of some absurd bedroom farce, both men said in unison, "What could I have done to make you happy?"

Larry put down his cards and stared at his friend. Friend? Could he even say that anymore?

"Nothing. It's my fault, I think." Sarah tapped her fingertips on the table. "Maybe I need some time to myself."

This was his chance. "Do you want a divorce?"

"No." There was no hesitation in her answer.

They both looked at Sarah.

Larry sucked in his breath. "Really?"

"Nah." Her fitness band buzzed. "I've gotta go check on the chicken." She put her cards down. "I'm done." She stood up, pushed in her chair, and trotted off.

Larry eyed Dougie, who looked like he was about to rupture a blood vessel. He gave him a minute to compose himself.

"Lah, I don't know what happened. I mean, her head didn't hit the dashboard or nothing like that. We weren't even going that fast. But she had a, whaddaya call it? An experience or something. Father and Sister What's Their Faces started talking to her."

"An experience? Do you mean an epiphany?"

"Right, yeah, an epiphany. We come back here and she's going through some old shit in her bedroom closet. She pulls out this prayer book she got when she was born or something. She tore through that thing, talking to herself. And then she got this funny look on her face."

"What kind of funny look?"

Dougie attempted to mimic Sarah's expression.

"You look constipated," Larry said.

Dougie gave up and shrugged his shoulders. "All I know is, we didn't go to bed today. We haven't been to bed in, like, two weeks." He sighed. "I don't know, but something's been happening with her."

"I'm done." Larry put his cards down.

Sarah returned with plates of food. She put one down on her place mat and the other at Dougie's.

"Oh, I'm sorry. Should I leave?" Larry's voice dripped with sarcasm.

"No, Dougie will," Sarah said.

Dougie popped up out of his chair like an obedient schoolboy.

Sarah looked at Larry. "I made dinner for you." She sounded penitent. Perhaps Dougie was right. But what the hell had happened?

"What the hell happened, Sarah?"

"I've made mistakes, Larry."

He moistened his lips and asked again. "Do you want a divorce?"

She either didn't hear him or chose to ignore him.

"And I know I can't erase my mistakes."

Dougie stood there enthralled, his jacket half on and mouth half open, eyes swiveling back and forth like he was at a tennis match and wanted both players to win.

Larry felt like he was having an out-of-body experience.

"But I can fix things. I can be a better wife to you. Starting right now." Sarah's wrist buzzed again, and she touched a button on the band to silence it. "That would be the pie."

Larry twitched. What kind of pie? He made a silent wish for apple.

"Lah, want to go to the brewery later?"

"Get the hell out of here, Dougie."

"Sure thing." Dougie zipped up his jacket and left.

Sarah came back with an apple crumb pie that looked like it belonged on the cover of a cookbook.

"Your favorite, right?"

It sure was.

Her fitness band beeped yet again. Jesus Christ, what now?

"Whoops. Time for church." She placed the pie on the table and went to the closet to get her coat. "Sorry, I can't stay to eat." She leaned over and blew out the candle on her side of the table. "But when I come back, you and I are going to the brewery."

"Um, okay. Wait, you're going to church? It's Thursday."

"Weekly novena. Enjoy your veal, hon."

Hon. This time, he heard it loud and clear.

She kissed him on his cheek and left the scent of her perfume. Was that for his benefit, or did she dab it on earlier for Dougie? Did he even want to know the answer to that question?

He heard the front door shut. He rubbed his forehead, then his temples. Then his stomach rumbled. He stared at his food. He picked up his fork, then slammed it down.

What a day.

He scratched his chest and remembered.

What a life.

He couldn't get Dougie's dumb face out of his head. He picked up his fork and tried to eat. Sarah had made this for him, not for Dougie. That was something. It was delicious—chicken marsala was her signature dish.

After he finished dinner, he cleaned up the dishes and took a shower. He shaved. He had been thinking about growing a beard, but that morning he'd noticed a gray coming in among the rest of the dark hairs on his chin. He'd considered plucking it but opted for a swipe of the razor instead.

He dressed in a pair of jeans and a sweater. He held his breath as he pulled it over his head, but it covered the lanyard well. It felt weird to be wearing anything besides work clothes or pajamas. He had been in a funk for so long. No wonder Sarah had taken up with Dougie.

But here they were. Going out on a date. He felt a familiar stirring in his stomach. Butterflies? Was he nervous about spending time with his wife? Yes, he was.

—

Sarah texted that she was back from church and waiting for him in the parking lot. Larry threw on his jacket, locked the door behind him, and took the elevator downstairs.

It was cold out, but there was no wind. It was the type of night that made winter bearable in New York. That is, until Sarah slid on some black ice as she stepped off the curb. She would have wiped out had he not been there to grab her.

"Whoa." They gave each other an awkward hug.

He was willing to take her to the city, to this fancy dessert place she had always wanted to go. He attempted to argue that going to the same place Dougie had asked him to go didn't constitute a date.

She waved a dismissive hand. "I think we both need a beer, Lah."

That he couldn't argue with.

They headed for the brewery located near their development, where they knew they could get some damn good beer. With the exception of Guinness, they didn't drink anything that was advertised on a Super Bowl commercial. When the brewery opened about a year ago, they were the first in line to get in.

They flashed their IDs to the guy at the door and bought four drink tickets. They walked to the bar and ordered pints of the new stout they had on tap.

They grabbed seats at a small table in the corner.

"So, what's new?" She sipped the foam from her glass. He choked on the foam in his.

Someone behind the bar dropped a tray of pint glasses and they shattered. Everyone in the place cheered. Someone shouted, "Opa!" like they were at a Greek wedding.

He recovered from his coughing fit. She tried again. "How have you been?"

It was a question that you'd ask someone who you hadn't seen in a while. An easy question to get the conversation going. Not something that you'd ask your spouse with whom you'd been living the entire time under the same roof.

"Well, it's been—" He took a gulp of the cold beer.

A dart whizzed by and buried itself in the wall next to them. Sarah's eyes went wide. Larry choked again.

A muffled expletive came from nearby, and the shuffling of feet. "Oh, my bad, my bad, my bad."

A tall, hulking man in an oversized flannel shirt and a bushy beard stood beside their table. Larry's neck hurt to look up at him.

"Wow, that would have been tragic," Flannel Shirt said. He dumped a handful of drink tickets on their table. "Here you go. My bad, guys."

Sarah pulled the dart out of the wall and gave it back to Flannel Shirt. "You should be glad we like beer, dude."

"I'll stick to foosball from now on. It's safer." Flannel Shirt returned to his group by the dartboard.

Larry looked at Sarah. They both looked at the pile of drink tickets, then back at each other.

"What do you think?" she said.

"Game on."

They downed their beers and went up to get more. This might turn out to be a good night after all.

She made him laugh about one of her clients who insisted on expensive shag carpeting throughout the whole house even though he had just gotten a new puppy and it was bound to be a disaster. He made her laugh about one of his clients who tried to write off his wife's spa treatments as a business expense, because the only way he could get any work done was if she wasn't around. Their conversation reminded him how each of them was in their own separate worlds for at least eight hours a day, five days a week. No wonder people drifted apart.

He gulped down the rest of his pint glass. She let out a little whoop, jumped up, and ran over to the bar with two more drink tickets.

Two rounds later, one of the bartenders stepped up to the microphone that was set up on the small stage in the front of the brewery.

"Test one two, test one two."

Larry winced as the microphone screeched.

"Is tonight what I think it is?" Sarah's eyes looked like they were about to pop out of her head.

"What's up everyone?" the bartender said. "It's karaoke night!"

A small smattering of applause. Sarah hooted.

"You'll sing with me, right, Lah?" she said, her words slurring a bit.

He needed more beer for sure. They had made a dent in the pile of beer tickets, but there were still a bunch left. Had Dart Guy come by with more as penance?

The room was getting fuzzy, but not fuzzy enough for him to want to grab a microphone. He walked over to the bar, got two more pints, and brought them back.

Sarah made him clink glasses, and she yelled, "Karaoke!"

One of Flannel Shirt's friends got up first and sang a song that Larry didn't recognize, but Sarah danced on her stool and mouthed along to the lyrics.

Another woman from the group went up next. Sarah drummed her palms against the table. "You know what song I want, right?"

"Ugh. Can't you pick another?"

"Noooooo." She shook her head, a flurry of blonde hair and that smile.

"Fine. Let's get this over with." They waited for the applause to die down for the second singer, then they walked to the stage.

Larry knew from early on in their relationship that karaoke

was part of the deal of being with Sarah. But he much preferred it when she sang by herself and he could cheer her on from the darkened seating area. But she had convinced him to join her for duets from time to time, often with Dougie heckling them from the audience. It had all been in good fun.

The guy queued up the track and handed them both a mike. Sarah bounced up on stage. "You ready?" she said into the microphone. The crowd cheered.

Larry planted his feet, trying hard to stay upright. So far, so good.

The music started. She chose "Love Nest," like she always did. It was one of those country music crossover duets that had been popular the year they got engaged. Larry had to work hard to convince her not to make this their wedding song. Instead, it became the highlight of her karaoke repertoire. Or rather, their repertoire. They had sung the duet together at least a dozen times during the course of their relationship. He did wish, though, that she'd let him sing the male parts of the song. She had a wacky sense of humor that didn't always translate well. But she was adamant. "People will get it and they'll love it," she would say.

She took in a big gulp of air and launched into the opening verse. The people at the tables by the front of the stage got it. They laughed and raised their pint glasses. Larry and Sarah were the fun couple in the room once more.

The lyrics flashed on the screen at the foot of the stage, but they both knew the words.

Fly on over to my love nest
You're the one who knows me best
Birds of a feather, we belong together
Our love will outshine the rest.

God, the lyrics were awful. They did sound much better against a retro '80s beat, but seeing them flash across the screen in block letters was borderline offensive. Even he, a numbers guy, could write better than that drivel. How much did it cost to put out a record, anyway? It had to be far less than five hundred seventy-five million dollars. Could he be a music producer? The image of him standing behind the control panel at a recording studio almost made him miss his cue.

The thing about karaoke was that you needed to choose a song the crowd knew well enough to get them to sing along and mask how bad you were. Sarah had a decent voice, but he was tone deaf, so he was happy to have the audience help. When they got to the chorus, he pointed the microphone at the crowd and they did the work for him. By now, he felt all six (seven? eight?) beers he had downed. The room took on that end-of-the-evening wobble that he hadn't experienced in a very long time.

Sarah smiled and bounced. He knew her favorite line was coming up, the one where the music stops for a few seconds and the female singer screeches the line that makes everyone in the music video laugh. But by flipping the script on their duet, it would be his turn in the spotlight. She gestured to the crowd—hush, hush, the best part was coming.

The music cut out and Sarah pointed to him.

He glanced at the monitor, even though he knew the next line. Of course he knew it. Everyone did. *I'm lucky because I'm the one you love.* He gripped the microphone tighter and howled.

"I'M LUCKY BECAUSE I'M THE ONE WHO WON THE LOTTERY!"

There was complete silence. Wow, the break in the music was longer than he remembered.

Sarah stared at him, mouth wide open.

Shit.

"Juuust kidding," he mumbled into the microphone.

The music resumed and the whole place cackled, just like the people did in the music video. Even Sarah was doubled over laughing. And just like that, everyone forgot what Larry said. Thank God for the short-term memory of drunk people.

He left her prancing around the stage for the last notes of the song and ran back to their table to grab their coats. They pulled them on, then she jumped onto his back for a piggyback ride. She flashed the room the peace sign and threw the rest of their drink tickets at the crowd. Everyone roared in approval. It was a great night.

With Sarah's giggles in his ear, they danced their way home. They burst into the building laughing. They startled the doorman at the desk. He saluted and mumbled something like "young love" as they tripped into the elevator.

"That was fun," she said. It came out as a gasp. "And you're hilarious." She swatted at his arm but missed. "I'm lucky because I'm the one who won the lottery," she said, mimicking his deep voice. "As if you ever played the lottery a day in your life."

The elevator opened and her laughter echoed in the empty hallway. She clapped a hand over her mouth. "Shh, this is a library," she said in a stage whisper.

They stumbled down the hallway to their door. She had to stop every so often to regain her balance. She tried to stifle her laughter, which came out instead as snorts. Tears streamed down her face.

He unlocked the door and shut it behind them. Their hands touched as they both reached for the lock. They slid the chain together and kept their hands there for a moment.

There was a flurry of hats, scarves, and jackets. The cold weather made things so difficult sometimes. He removed his sweater as she slipped out of hers.

Shit. The lanyard.

She grabbed it from around his neck and slid it over his head.

"No need for office IDs. You are most certainly off the clock."

Moshertainly off the clock.

To his horror, she attempted to wrap the lanyard around her neck like a boa, but it was too short. She whirled it above her head, then marched down the hallway to their bedroom as if she were leading a parade. The lanyard flew off her fingers. He grabbed it, his heart pounding. He ran back for his coat and zipped the ticket away into a pocket, then followed her into the bedroom, stumbling over the pile of clothes she had shed.

She turned to him.

God, she was beautiful.

"Do you want to?" she asked.

"Yes."

She leapt onto the bed. She reached out to him, grabbed the waistband of his jeans, and pulled him into an embrace. Her kisses felt strange and familiar all at once. He tried not to think of when Dougie had last kissed her. Maybe none of that mattered anymore.

She nuzzled his ear. "Oh, Larry."

His name never sounded sexy until she said it.

"Oh, Monica."

Oh, no.

She pulled back. Her confusion was soon replaced with anger then sadness, and then, of all things, a smile. That same angelic smile she had on her face when she was talking about the priest and the nun.

"Sarah, I didn't mean—"

She put out a hand to stop him.

"S'okay. I deserve this," she said, then collapsed face down on the bed.

He pulled the cover up over her as she started to snore.

He went around his side of the bed, stripped down to his boxers, and climbed in. Then he got out of bed again, ran for his coat that was still in the hallway by the door. He grabbed the lanyard, tucked it away in the pocket of a pair of slacks.

His heavy eyelids closed, and at last, this crazy day was over.

Chapter 12

The next day, Larry's head throbbed. He stared at his computer screen, trying to make sense of whatever it was Jordan had done to one of his client's spreadsheets.

The hair pricked up along the back of his neck.

Was someone staring at him?

He looked up.

Everyone was staring at him.

His eyelid twitched. "Can I help someone?"

Irving cleared his throat and cocked his head at the door.

Monica.

All eyes shifted to her.

She looked pleased. She was used to people looking at her.

But she was looking at him right now.

"Lunch?"

He smiled, and his hangover was forgotten.

They sat in a booth by the front window at the Queen's Court Diner, the same one they had sat in many times in college. In fact, the same hostess from back then still worked there. God, how old was she? Instead of walking them to their table like she used to, she pointed to it with a smile.

It was strange not to have seen Monica for so many years—well, in person, anyway—and now to be seated across from her. Unlike those simpler times, they sat in silence as they looked at the menus. It struck him as odd. There had to be so much they could say to each other. But he had no idea where to start. Maybe lunch had been a bad idea. Maybe they should have gone for coffee instead. But this was not a first date. This was a reunion between two old friends, right?

He picked up a couple of packets of sugar and shook them like maracas.

She tapped her shiny red nails against the table.

"How's Hannah?" she said.

"Hannah?"

"Your wife?"

"You mean Sarah."

"Of course. Sorry. Where did I get Hannah from?"

"Sarah's fine. We're both doing fine."

More silence.

He studied the salt and pepper shakers. He grabbed them and tightened the tops. Sure enough, the one on the saltshaker was loose. Some idiot kid still found it funny to loosen the caps so that some poor soul would have an avalanche of salt on their food. Old-school Staten Island pranks.

"What have you been up to?" he asked.

"Well, I've—"

"That's a ridiculous question."

She raised an eyebrow.

"I read the news. I know what you're up to. All of Staten Island knows what you're up to. Well, even more than Staten Island. I was in Jersey once at this convenience store? Saw a pile of *Advances* there right next to the *Asbury Park Press*, so I'm thinking that part of the Garden State knows what you've been up to, too."

She flicked her hair over her shoulder and smiled. "You've been following."

He looked down. He was never good at playing it cool. He laughed in spite of himself. "You caught me. Guess I have been. But who can keep up with you? Every other day, your picture is in the paper. Or Max's. You're both so photogenic."

She smiled. Her teeth were pure white. Bleached? Capped? Had to be one or the other. Teeth that white and straight did not exist in nature.

"So, how are you?"

"I'm spectacular." She sniffled. Then she started to cry. She shielded her face with one hand and reached into her purse with the other to grab a tissue. She blotted her eyes. The tissue came away black, smudged with mascara.

A waitress brought their coffee. He took a sip. It was as terrible as he remembered, but at least the caffeine would soothe his headache. He swallowed some more.

For the next ten minutes, he dragged a spoon around his mug in slow circles as he listened to her talk about what it was like being married to Max Rossi. Well, it was more like she was talking to the digital jukebox perched on the wall of their booth. Like the old-fashioned one that held 45 rpm records, this digital version displayed album listings on pages that could be flipped by the turn of a dial. She hid her face as she studied the song list. She cranked the dial so hard she almost broke a nail. She stopped to examine it, then scrolled again. Hundreds of tunes about love and heartbreak waiting to be played with the swipe of a credit card. These jukeboxes hadn't accepted coins in over a decade.

"At first, it was nothing. Max and I would give a little here. We'd go to a couple of fundraisers there. Well, we must have picked all the right charities and all the right fundraisers because next thing you know we were asked to do stuff all the time. 'Please cut this ribbon.' 'Please stand on this float.' Do you know local dress shops send me their stuff to wear like I'm a

Hollywood celebrity?"

He nodded as if he knew what the hell she was talking about, all the while trying to ignore the growls emerging from his stomach. He was famished, even though he had eaten a huge breakfast sandwich a couple of hours ago. He tried to catch their server's eye. He was afraid this might make him appear rude, but then again, Monica wasn't even looking at him. Her attention was still on the jukebox.

"It's like I'm Miss America, except my reign keeps going on and on and on." More sniffling, more scrolling.

"Careful what you wish for."

"What?" She paused for a second and looked at him. Her eyes were misty and red, her face a delicate, bruised flower. She blew her nose in a napkin. It sounded like the foghorn on the Staten Island Ferry. Their waitress behind the counter looked up, startled. When she saw the sound was emanating from Monica, she smiled and brought over a stack of napkins.

Larry cleared his throat. "Nah, it's nothing." He glanced at the album page she had paused on. He cocked his head at the CD. It was *The Best of What's Around, Vol. 1* by Dave Matthews Band. "Remember?"

It was 1998. They had gone to see them at Madison Square Garden. DMB was playing one of their popular ballads. The crowd seemed to shrink as couples stepped into various embraces and clinches, hands grabbing hands and arms wrapping around shoulders in the darkness.

It was their first official date, and he was dying to kiss her. He took a step toward her as she turned to him. A lump formed in his throat as he looked down at her. Her hand slid up his chest to his cheek. She let it rest there for a moment before she pulled his face toward hers.

They kissed. He had been prepared for fireworks and bottle rockets, but it was sloppy, a complete dud. They missed each other's mouths. Monica giggled. They tried again. This time, they aligned lips. It was better, but still nothing to curl Larry's toes. *What the hell?* He thought he was a good kisser, had been told as much by his high school girlfriend, even though she eventually dumped him.

"Remember what?" She had a blank, beautiful stare. Her damp blue eyes sparkled.

"Nah, nothing."

The waitress brought their food. The tuna club with fries for him. A salad with the dressing on the side for her.

They ate in companionable silence. She didn't ask about his life, his home, his marriage. Which was fine because he didn't know where to begin.

When the check arrived, he grabbed it.

"Hey, I invited you."

"C'mon. I'm a gentleman."

"Yes, now I remember." They looked at each other. For that moment, he felt like he was back in college, when it was hard to look too long at Monica without wanting to take her back to his dorm room after class. Which he never had the guts to do.

The hostess plucked the check from his grip. "So sorry, Mrs. Rossi. I didn't recognize you earlier. Owner says it's on the house. Take care." She walked away.

Larry looked at Monica, then at his empty hand.

"I'll leave a nice tip." He pulled out his billfold and dropped a twenty on the table.

At the door, he saw Dougie. He was with a work buddy, as evidenced by their matching dark gray cargo pants and polo shirts. Larry willed them to look in any direction but theirs, but Dougie saw them. He did a double take, then he glared.

Larry raised an eyebrow in response. No use ignoring him. He had nothing to hide being out to lunch with Monica. Besides, he didn't care what Dougie thought. Or anyone else, for that matter.

Was that what being rich was like?

Chapter 13

Jordan was right about one thing: Larry would choose the lump sum payout of his lottery winnings. The newspapers, when they weren't speculating about the identity of the Staten Island winner, had mentioned time and again that this was one of the biggest payouts to a single winner in the history of Power Payday. He wasn't sure if this meant another bonus tax bracket. Damn IRS.

He estimated the payout to be around thirty-five hundred times his annual salary at Parker & Rosenthal, which meant it was about nine thousand times his salary at Island Tax Prep. He popped two more antacid tablets.

He was not an adventurous type of guy, so he knew that he would never find himself in a situation where he was hurtling down a waterfall, clinging to a capsized canoe, or escaping a reptile attack. But even in disaster fantasies, he envisioned himself as the level-headed person who would save the day. So why was it so damn hard for him to wrap his head around winning the lottery? It wasn't life or death. It was just money.

To be sure, winning the lottery had a lot more inherent pleasure and excitement than, say, being chased up a tree in the African savanna by a lion. In his research, he had found out that the latter scenario was statistically more plausible than a lottery win, but that was beside the point.

He wiped his brow. Was it possible for his brain to sweat? He wondered if this was what Dougie experienced whenever he tried to figure something out. Thinking was his cardio.

Larry sat down at the desk in his home office and slid open the drawer. He pulled out the floor plan and unfolded it. He had forgotten to update it last month with the latest mortgage payment. They must have paid off at least another square foot of something.

But now.

He could have taken the highlighter and swiped it across the page with abandon, like a wild child set loose with a coloring book. He could have lit it on fire or flushed it down the toilet. He envisioned himself folding it into an origami swan that he could float across New York Harbor. He wouldn't need to color in a floorplan anymore. This would be their home, free and clear. Even though it looked like only one of them would continue to live there.

This kingdom would be his, far sooner than he'd ever imagined. Security and the American Dream would be his too, now and forever. He didn't have a clue what to do with any of it.

Larry Sortino. Insecure about security. He wanted to punch himself in the face.

He'd begun to question everything he thought he knew about money and how it should be spent or saved. When he worked with his super rich clients, those who could afford to own multiple properties, he knew better than to advise them to pay off any of those mortgages in full. In any economy, up or down, the clear advantage was still on the side of the homeowner. The tax benefits of a mortgage were too good.

It would make sense for him to do something similar when

he was ready to venture into real estate investments. But he balked at his own advice. Why? He did not want to give up this chance to own his kingdom outright. He would pay off the mortgage. He could look up the final payoff figure through his online account and then transfer the money. Better yet, he would do it in person. Something this monumental was worth a trip to the bank and the paper for an actual check.

After he paid off the condo, he would buy another home. Then another. He would be like that actress who collected castles, buying a new one with each starring role. Or maybe not. He recalled reading somewhere that she had foreclosed on half of her real estate portfolio. She had dried up in Hollywood, and so had her moats.

Fine, so he wouldn't buy castles. He would stick to houses and condos.

But first, he would have to get up the guts to claim the damn prize.

A big part of the reason he enjoyed his scratch-off games was that they promised miniature thrills. Winning a few bucks here or there was nothing over the top, nothing he couldn't handle. It was a thrill on par with, say, the first time he and Dougie rode the Cyclone at Coney Island when they were kids. He might have been worried for a second or two that they were going to fly out of the car and land on top of the roof of Nathan's Famous, but after that, it was loads of fun.

Even if Larry had hit the top jackpot of the Made in the Shade game, he'd had a five-year plan. He would continue to work while he banked three thousand a week (around seventeen hundred after taxes) and plan his next steps. He would have Sarah by his side, perhaps a little one, too. That was all. All he needed, all he wanted.

Tiny prizes, tiny thrills. Finances he could wrap his head around. He could still be his own accountant, still be able to look at his checkbook (yes, he still had an actual checkbook, even in the digital banking age) and know that his monkey brain could make sense of the numbers written on the ledger.

Oh, but *now*.

There was a reason Parker & Rosenthal put whole teams of accountants on big clients. That many zeros required that many more sets of eyes. It made perfect sense. When the wealth was that vast, more brain power was needed.

His head swam. This time, the zeros belonged to him—or would belong to him in due time—and he had no one to help him. Or rather, he had plenty of people he could hire to help him, but who could he trust? Who could he even tell?

What the hell was he going to do?

His hands tightened into fists. Clench, unclench. Clench, unclench. He had just trimmed his nails, but their edges still made crescent-shaped indentations into his palms.

It was a shame that New York didn't allow lottery winners to remain anonymous. He supposed it was because the state had too many other issues to deal with. It was understandable that lawmakers didn't have the time or inclination to include lottery winner rights in their orders of business when they had much more important things to contend with like marriage equality and affordable housing.

Lawyers. He would need one, maybe even several. The unhappily-ever-after lottery winner stories that Jordan and Irving had laughed about haunted him. He would need a legal strategy to protect him and his money.

He scoured the internet for more evidence of people who made a mess out of their lives after winning. And he found plenty. So many people did weird things when vast sums of money came into their lives. They would invest in companies that toppled like houses of cards. They purchased mansions that cost millions to maintain. They bought boats. And then they lost it all. He might not have earned the money in the first place, but he would make it his job to avoid acting like a damn fool now that he had it.

When he accepted his position at Parker & Rosenthal fifteen

years ago, his mother had raised her well-groomed eyebrows at his starting salary. He had searched the newspaper every day for apartment listings in Manhattan. The rents made him hyperventilate, so he'd tried Brooklyn. Those rents were a bit better, but it would mean a longer commute, almost as long as he would have had if he'd stayed on Staten Island. Which is what he did. He found a small one-bedroom in a two-family house in St. George, just a few blocks to the ferry.

His mother had wanted him to stay home. "Do it for a year," she said. "Save up some money. Start your retirement fund. You are going to take advantage of that company match, Larry. You've got your retirement to think of."

"Ma, I'm twenty-two," he said.

His mother gave him a look that only a mother of an insolent son fresh out of college can give.

"Just because you've got some money now doesn't mean you have to act like an ass."

She'd been right. He wondered what she would say to him now.

Maybe not everyone acted like asses when they came into money. But it was fair to say most of them did. Still, he had higher hopes for himself.

Chapter 14

One morning, Larry awoke to an alert on his phone. A local news headline flashed across the fractured screen. He still hadn't gone to the mall to get a new one.

YOU WON THE LOTTERY!

He squinted at the headline again.

WHO WON THE LOTTERY?

Oh. That was better. But not by much.

The article featured an exterior photo of the Bay Street Mini Mart. Sunil was there with a big smile, standing beside another man with a similar smile. He looked closer. It was Gaurav. Larry almost didn't recognize him without his smirk. Still, it made sense. Gaurav had every reason to be happy—the Gaming Commission always gave the winning store a cash prize.

He stared at the headline again. It posed a question that might inspire lighthearted chatter around the proverbial water coolers. But for him, it was a warning. To him, it said, "It's just a matter of time before we find out who you are."

He needed a plan.

With gentle swipes of his pinky, he opened the calendar app on his phone. He frowned and squinted at the small dates on the grid. He preferred to keep track of his schedule on actual paper with an actual pen, but he liked the safety of being able to lock his phone screen. Besides, a calendar was another thing to worry about hiding. But after he sliced the tip of his finger again on the screen, he gave up. He rummaged through his desk and took out the small pocket datebook he had gotten in his Parker & Rosenthal holiday gift bag last year.

It had been just three weeks since he'd won, but it might as well have been three months. He was losing track of time, and he couldn't afford to. By law, winners had a year from the date on the winning ticket to come forward. Resident lottery expert Jordan had said as much, and Larry even confirmed it on the Gaming Commission's website.

He opened the slim calendar and stared at the dates. The fact that he had forty-nine more weeks to hatch a plan to claim the prize in as low-profile a way as possible made him feel like he could breathe again.

The calendar would help him figure out what he needed to do and when. He wasn't stupid enough to write down CLAIM PRIZE or BECOME RICH TODAY on any calendar, of course. He would be far more cryptic than that. He'd write something like 10K RACE, a fitness goal that wouldn't be out of the question for him to work toward. He had run a bit years ago when he and Sarah started dating. She'd told him he had good form. That had to count for something.

Yes. That's what he would do. He would mark his calendar with exercise milestones that would serve as code for his tasks for claiming the money. He would have to look up what it meant to train for a 10K, though. He had no idea about running terminology. Sarah would say, "I'm going for a run," and off she went. How complicated could it be?

Ugh. He remembered that many of Sarah's recent "runs" weren't athletic in nature. So he couldn't trust anything she said. Running? Stretching? Yoga? All could have had a double meaning. What a fool he'd been.

He chose a date a few weeks out and wrote JOIN A RUNNING CLUB. This meant that he was going to find a lawyer who specialized in prize money.

He chose another date. GET NEW SNEAKERS. This meant that he would find another place to hide his ticket. The lanyard was starting to chafe his neck.

SIGN UP FOR A 5K CHARITY RACE. This meant that he would research charities to see which ones he wanted to support.

SCHEDULE A MASSAGE. He didn't know what this one would mean yet, but it made sense in the running context. Perhaps it would refer to something important, like a call with his would-be lawyer or something. Maybe he would go for an actual massage. Or maybe he would start an actual workout routine. His appetite had returned with a vengeance, and he was gaining weight.

The neighborhood bank wouldn't cut it anymore. He would have to get on a first-name basis with an investment firm. What would that conversation be like? "Hi, I'm rich now, please help."

He would need a place to live. Investing in more real estate had always been part of the dream, but he figured it to be a long-term strategy. Now, he would need to find another place as soon as possible. Living with Sarah was getting to be too weird.

Would he leave New York? He didn't want to. This was his home. But maybe a change in scenery would do him good. He didn't care to be gawked at in public for the rest of his life. He assumed that's what other people did when local lottery winners were in their midst. He would have to move. People would always say, "I'm moving to an island," when they wanted to get away from it all. He already was on an island. Maybe he could buy one of his own? Were there real estate agents for that sort of thing? Ugh, add another item to his research list.

He began to sweat like he was actually running a 10K. He snorted whenever he thought about Jordan's plan for winning.

Cars, vacations, and a middle finger to everyone who wronged him? Jordan would be toast. He would end up as the main character in one of those unhappily-ever-after stories he and Irving were so fond of sharing.

He would not be like Jordan.

He went into the bathroom and splashed some cold water on his face. Then he did it again. Then again.

He hated carrying around this terrible secret. Okay, so maybe "terrible" wasn't the right word. He wasn't a criminal, although he felt like one. How did criminals live with themselves? He remembered that old crime drama series, starring a bumbling, cigar-smoking detective in a beat-up leather jacket who always got his guy. Toward the end of every episode, the perps would confess to everything, sure that they were about to get away with it all. They never did, because the detective wasn't bumbling at all—he was always a step or two ahead. Still, in each episode, the perp spilled all his or her dark deeds in a confessional monologue. But there was no redemption for them, just handcuffs and a strange sense of relief. They were tired of being on the run. He could sympathize.

He took out his phone and swiped open the screen, cursing as the sharp edge of the cracked glass sliced at his fingertips yet again.

He launched a meditation app he had heard about on TV and started his breathing exercises. Every day for the past week, he'd set aside a few minutes to focus on inhaling and exhaling to the gentle beat of rainfall. "April Showers" was the name of the setting. He tried not to feel angry that he needed to be reminded to breathe. But this dumb little app was the one thing that was keeping him sane. It kept him from blurting out "IT WAS ME! I WON!" when anyone looked at him at work.

He completed the exercises and felt calmer.

He got out a pen and flipped to the back of the datebook to the next year's calendar on a two-page spread. He tapped his index finger on January three times. Then he put a circle around the 31st, the day he won the lottery.

His pulse quickened.

He slashed his pen through the date. He couldn't claim it on the *anniversary* of his win. It would have to be the day earlier. The anniversary would be the 366th day, not the 365th!

He remembered that this was a leap year. Did the Gaming Commission take that into account? Would it be okay if the lottery winner had 366 days to claim instead of 365? The drawing was done late at night, so did that mean that he was a winner at the moment of the drawing? Did the next day count as Day 1 or Day 2?

Now, it was like he hadn't done the breathing exercises at all. He forced himself to focus—in through the nose, out through the mouth.

He would claim it a bit earlier. He looked at the January grid and circled January 24, a week shy of the deadline. He frowned. He knew the tax laws for this year. But how would they affect him next year?

He turned back a page to the month of December and started to circle December 31. But, no, that wouldn't work. What if they closed early for the holidays? What if they were closed for the entire week of Christmas?

Fine, November. He circled the Friday of the week before Thanksgiving. There. That was his D-Day.

He was as exhausted as if he had actually completed one of his alleged training runs. But he was also satisfied. Ten months—no, make that nine—was plenty of time to do whatever it was he would need to do.

His head swam. He reached for his phone, winced as the screen scraped at the same spot on his finger, and launched the meditation app again. "April Showers" wouldn't do it for him this time around. He scrolled through the other themes and landed on "Rain in the Amazon." In seconds, he was transported to the rainforest, but instead of the soft drumbeat of the raindrops, he heard the squawks of some jungle bird. Breathe in—squawk.

Breathe out—squawk. How could this be relaxing? He decided he'd had enough of rainstorms. This time, he chose "Santorini Seashore" and settled into waves crashing upon the sand. Much better. As long as no chatty seabirds announced themselves, he could continue to breathe.

What a farce his life had become. Did he really need nine months to claim a lottery prize? Of course not. In the past week, he had scoured the internet and found dozens of articles about recent lottery winners. The longest it had taken any of them to come forward was a week. But those jackpots were much smaller than his. The one win that got anywhere close to his prize amount was a shared jackpot. He should be so lucky that his name could blend into a long list of other names, like the credits at the end of a movie.

But no. He had to be the sole winner this time around. He hoped that there would be an announcement of another winner. Perhaps someone from some tiny, out-of-the-way town that had a country store, not a convenience store. A store so remote it didn't have internet access, so the owner didn't know a customer had won. But Jordan had nixed that notion. Farmers could get internet access, too, he said. Plus the Gaming Commission knew where every winning ticket was sold.

He was screwed. He would have to claim the ticket under his own name, not Jim Wingersfield (a name he had been toying with). Everyone would know he won. Everyone would know him.

They'd probably know Sarah, too. She would get half of the prize money. That was a given. He wasn't worried about it. He imagined them buying a house large enough so that they could have his-and-her wings, if she still insisted on no divorce. It seemed that she did want to stay married and not drive off into the sunset with Dougie. That dingleberry. There was no way he was getting any of Larry's money. All right, maybe, for old time's sake, but just a little.

It was all so very complicated. Whoever said that money

was supposed to make things easier was a damn fool. Larry had made unfair assumptions about rich people in the past. He supposed it was fair that people would now make assumptions about him. He knew people would consider him a miserable shit if he didn't give money to his best friend, regardless of who was the actual shit in the equation. When this level of money was involved, common sense no longer prevailed.

Damn it all to hell. This was supposed to be easy. It was supposed to be fun.

Chapter 15

The new Varma Convenience Store at last opened next door to the Island Tax Prep office. At first, Larry felt weird about going there, like he was cheating on Sunil and Gaurav. Well, maybe just Sunil. He didn't care how Gaurav felt about anything.

Although the store was about the same size as the Bay Street Mini Mart, nothing was in the same place. The first few times he went in, he felt like an idiot wandering the aisles in search of a snack or the iced tea that he liked. There was no rhyme or reason to the candy aisle. Here, the candy was arranged by type—the owner wasn't a heathen, after all—but it was alphabet soup among the gum and chocolate bars. He gave up on the peanut caramel bar he wanted and instead took a package of red licorice that was somehow placed next to the lollipops.

Fine. Different store, different rules. The shop owner was a very serious-looking man. He had his daughter working alongside him in the afternoons, a slim, pretty young woman with long dark hair that she wore in some complicated braid. He was never good with guessing people's ages, but she wore a

Wagner College hoodie over her Catholic school skirt. Larry felt confident enough in those clues to ask her if she was going to Wagner in the fall.

She smiled and nodded her head, her braid bobbing behind her neck.

"My wife and I are alumni," he said.

Her face lit up. "You are? What were your majors?"

"She majored in arts administration and I was accounting. Do you know what you want to study yet?"

"Finance."

Interesting. Just like Gaurav. Larry had a fleeting image of that sullen twenty-something as a teenager in high school. Was he the same back then, or had he once been as sweet as this young woman? Could it be that all those years of studying forecasts and budgets and quantitative analysis turned you into an asshole? Accounting was related to finance, but there was a difference. Larry didn't think he was an asshole, but then again, did assholes self-identify as such?

"Sir?"

"Hmm?"

The young woman stared at him, eyebrows raised.

"I asked you if you were a CPA."

"Oh. Yes, I am. I work next door doing taxes. But I was at a firm in the city for many years."

"Oh, you got laid off? I'm sorry."

His foot kicked the bottom of the counter so hard that she jumped. He groaned.

"Are you okay?"

"Just dandy. Can I have twenty dollars of Made in the Shades, please?"

For a second, he marveled about how natural he sounded. No need for a fake voice, no need to wear the hat of a team he didn't root for. He hadn't even planned to buy tickets—he still had a stack of unopened ones in the console of his car.

"These are my favorite ones," she said to him after she

ripped the cards from the roll. "If I won, I could go to school and not worry about a job afterwards." Her eyes widened. "Oh, I don't mean I would be lazy, I just mean I'd work wherever I wanted to work."

"Sure, lots of options in finance."

"Finance, ugh." She stuck her tongue out in disgust.

"Didn't you say that's what you want to major in?"

"I'm going into finance so I can buy a house," she said. "Once I pay it off, then I can do whatever I want."

"I know all about it. But wouldn't it be better to study something that made you happy?"

"Nope. Happiness is knowing that my mortgage is paid off."

The bottle of iced tea slipped out of his hands and smashed on the floor. He felt the diet green tea and all of its antioxidants seep through the soles of his shoes.

"I'm so sorry." He was so mortified, he repeated it three times, almost like an incantation. Perhaps it was. On the third time, another employee appeared with a mop and a dustbin, and the glass and liquid were swept away, like it had never happened.

The girl behind the counter giggled. "No worries, sir."

"Please, call me Larry."

"Okay, well, I'm Natasha. You can go get another one, if you want."

He shook his head and waved his licorice. "This is more my speed today, I suppose." He ripped off one of the Made in the Shade cards and dropped it in the jar that had a neon pink sticky note on it that read TIPS FOR COLLEGE FUND in curly letters.

"Aww, you're so sweet," she said.

Natasha's dad walked by. He made a clucking noise with his tongue. "That jar is for real tips. No one wins those things."

"Why do you sell them, then?" Larry asked.

"No one seems to care that no one wins these things." His laughter boomed throughout the store.

"Please excuse my father," Natasha said. "Dad, this is Larry. He was an accounting major at Wagner."

"I'm a CPA," Larry said. He touched the licorice to his head like he was saluting the man.

"So he should know. Wagner is double the price since he went." The man looked at Larry as if the higher tuition was his fault.

Larry stammered yet another apology as he put a single in the jar. The man stared until he added another. The man's smile returned. "Good, support the next generation. She's going to work on Wall Street and give her daddy stock tips so he can retire rich."

"Great, and I'll get arrested for insider trading." Natasha rolled her eyes and laughed.

"I'll visit you every week in jail," her father said as he planted a kiss on her head.

Natasha reached her slender fingers into the jar and plucked out the Made in the Shade card. "Want your card back?"

"Nah, take it. Just for fun. And hey, if you do win, consider it the Larry Sortino Scholarship fund."

She put a hand to her chest and smiled.

His face burned. He could pay for that girl's college tuition in full without it making a dent in his jackpot money. He turned and walked toward the door. As he opened it, he looked down at the stack of newspapers in the stand. He saw a photo of Monica, who still managed to look radiant even in black and white. The caption said something about a fundraiser for some school. No picture of Max, just her.

Later, on his walk home after work, Larry checked the news headlines. Walking while he looked at his phone was a bad habit he'd picked up of late. He knew he was a pothole, curb, or pile of dog poop away from catastrophe.

As he waited for the light to change at Victory Boulevard and Bay Street, he heard a car honk. He looked up from his phone to see Dougie pull up to the curb with a stern look on his face. He pointed to his passenger seat.

Shit.

Larry walked over to the open passenger's side window. "Good evening, Dougie."

"You never told me your office moved. Get in."

"No thanks." The situation reminded him of one of those after-school specials on television. This episode would be titled something like, "Don't Take Candy from Strangers."

"Get in."

"What do you want, Dougie?"

"You were with Monica Rossi at the diner last week."

"Yes. Yes, I was."

"She's all over the place."

"I guess."

"What the hell is she doing with you?"

"Having lunch?"

"What about Sarah?"

Larry burst out laughing. He had never been one to laugh at anyone's expense, which was saying something considering all the ridiculous things Dougie had done or said over the years. But he could bite his tongue no longer.

"You are a pathetic little man," he said and got into the car. He wasn't giving in, but he didn't want to make a scene cackling at him on the street.

"Huh?" It never took much to confuse Dougie.

"You have the nerve to come here to ask me questions and patronize me when you're the one committing adultery. No, I mean cuckoldry." Ugh, now there was a word that he never hoped to use out loud in a sentence. Larry flexed his neck to the left and right, then again. He hoped it would make a crack like he'd seen countless times in movies when the tough guy was about to lay into the little guy, but his neck bones wouldn't cooperate. And Dougie was in too much of a daze to notice it. Maybe he was stumped by the word "cuckoldry."

Dougie stared at the dashboard. "I love Sarah."

"I am so sorry for you."

"She does things to me."

"Spare me." Larry started to feel sick to his stomach, even though the urge to laugh was still strong.

"I feel like I've screwed things up with her."

"Are you expecting me to give you relationship tips?"

Dougie sipped his coffee. "Got any?"

Unbelievable. He pointed to Dougie. "Screwing over his supposed best friend." He pointed at himself. "Not screwing over his supposed best friend."

Dougie sniffed, then started to cry.

"Oh jeez."

Dougie reached into the paper bag next to him. Larry assumed he was searching for a napkin, but he pulled out a cruller instead and took a bite. He looked pathetic.

"You screwed up everything, Dougie. You screwed my wife."

"I know. I'm an asshole."

"I won't argue that point."

Dougie reached into the bag again, this time for a crumpled napkin. He wiped his nose. "I've become one of those men, Lah. I wore two different boots to work the other day, and I didn't even realize until the new guy pointed it out to me."

"It happens."

Dougie shook his head. "I've been trying to get my shit together for a while now, and it's not working. I was banking on a promotion this time, but the budget is frozen. Next year, they promised me." He didn't sound convinced.

"Dougie, no one has their shit together. The world is an imperfect place."

Dougie let out a shaky sigh.

Larry himself had never cried over Sarah, ever. Not even during all the trouble they'd had conceiving. Not even now, when it had been made clear that she had fallen out of love with her husband for this guy, this blubbering sack of shit.

"You'll figure it all out," Larry said. "Or at least a good

portion of it."

Dougie took another bite of the cruller and sniffled again.

"But do me a favor, huh?"

Dougie took a deep breath. "Yeah?"

"Leave me out of it."

Dougie exhaled, as if he had expected a much bigger request.

Damn. He had missed another opportunity to ask for more, even if it were just the rest of Dougie's cruller. He would need to get better at that. He wondered what else the world might offer if he asked for things more often.

"Okay. You're a good friend, Lah. I don't deserve you."

"No, you don't." Larry got out and slammed the door.

Chapter 16

Jordan stormed in for his afternoon shift. He slammed his books on his desk.

Irving looked at Larry and shrugged.

"What's wrong, Jordan?" Larry asked.

No answer.

"Jordan?"

Jordan slumped down in his chair and rotated around inch by inch, to prolong the drama.

"I'm not working at the news station," he said.

"Yes, that's true. You're working at Island Tax Prep, your friendly neighborhood tax firm," Larry said in his best television announcer voice, as he took a pile of client folders from Irving.

Jordan glared at him.

"Whoa."

"I mean I didn't get that internship in the city. I got the 'Thanks, but go fuck yourself' email today. Oops." Jordan murmured an apology and glanced around the office, but at this time of day, there were no clients around. His rage returned and he slammed a fist on his desk.

Larry put down his pen.

"Probably went to some spoiled brat at Columbia J school. I'm gonna be stuck on stupid public access for the rest of my life. Even I can't remember what channel we're on." Jordan twirled the chair around again. It was a miracle the thing didn't come unscrewed and topple over.

Larry knew nothing about journalism, aside from reading the newspaper most days. His reading habits of late, though, had dwindled to a scan of the headlines with a sigh of relief when the lottery winner speculation stories—there was a new one just about every other day—came up empty. He was in no position to spout any wisdom about writing or reporting. But Jordan's struggle to get ahead in his career saddened him. His own professional trajectory was more linear, more assured. Major in accounting, become an accountant. Pass the CPA exam, become a CPA. Journalism was so different. Someone could hone their writing and reporting chops all they wanted, but they had to wait for that juicy story to come along and give them their big break.

"What did you have to do to apply for this internship?"

"I researched a topic and wrote an investigative report."

"Yeah? On what?"

"The recycling habits of my neighbors in our apartment building."

Larry considered this for a moment.

"Jordan, that's boring as hell."

"Oh, c'mon, Larry."

"Can't you find something more timely and exciting?"

"Sure, I'll just travel to Antarctica and cover global warming."

"I'm sure the kid from Columbia already thought of that."

Jordan flipped him the middle finger.

"I know, I deserve that. Listen, can you apply again?"

"They just announced a new summer internship."

"See? Another chance right around the corner."

Jordan waited for him to go on.

"Uh, where do you get ideas for your stories?"

"Newspaper headlines, social media."

"Nah, that's old news already. You've got to get out in front of the headlines."

Jordan looked inspired. Maybe Larry did know a little bit about what he was talking about after all. Wow. Is this how those fast-talking, self-anointed gurus filled up convention halls for those empowerment seminars?

"Find something that interests you, then get on the story before anyone else does," he said. "What interests you?"

Jordan chewed his lip. "People. Why they do the things they do."

"Great. They call that a human-interest story, right?"

"Yep."

"So, find an interesting human and do a story. There are a lot of them on the Island."

They both turned to look at the waiting area. A woman in a business suit sat in the corner, working on a laptop as she waited to be called. She wore a pair of headphones that made it look like she had gigantic cat ears.

"There are a lot of them in this office," Jordan said in a stage whisper. Larry cringed, but the kitten woman was none the wiser.

"There's a story out there. Find it. What's the worst that could happen?"

Jordan nodded and gave him a fist bump. He twirled back around in his chair and drummed his hands on the desk.

Larry tapped his right foot three times and smiled. He had done a good deed.

But unlike so many other good deeds, he was sure this one would remain unpunished.

—

He missed Manhattan. Sure, the city was crowded and noisy

and people never knew how to share the sidewalk, but it made him feel like he was part of something big every day. Working so close to home made him feel even more tense, like the world was closing in on him.

His ties were choking him. He had never minded them before, but a tie plus the lanyard was too much to bear. Perhaps it was time to take the ticket off for a little while. He lifted the lanyard over his head and wound it around the plastic, then knotted it. He fished around the top drawer of his nightstand until he found a safety pin, then secured the ticket inside the pocket of a pair of work slacks, which he hung in the darkest corner of his closet.

He pulled on a pair of track pants and a Yankees sweatshirt. It was cold, but not frigid out, so he zipped up a fleece jacket instead of his coat. He left the condo and walked at a brisk pace to the store, passing by Sarah's empty spot in the parking lot.

To keep anyone from finding out he was the winner, he had to maintain his routines, which included his regular trips to the convenience store for his scratch-off tickets. After all, Sunil and Gaurav knew someone won, but they didn't know it was him. He decided he would have to return to the Bay Street Mini Mart each week for his scratch-off tickets. Any fear that his presence would set off the security detectors was plain ridiculous, he decided.

He slowed his pace as he got closer. He did not look forward to seeing Gaurav. So much so that when he got to the store, he kept walking. He went a block, two blocks, three blocks. He was invigorated by the exercise in the chilly air. When he had walked about a mile past the store, he turned around and came back.

Sunil was behind the counter. No Gaurav in sight. No security alarm set off. What a relief. He greeted the store owner but didn't feel much like talking, so he listened to Sunil prattle on about how he couldn't believe the winner bought the ticket from his store. He paid, and when Sunil slid across the counter that small, nondescript paper bag of scratch-off cards, Larry put up his hand. He was about to tell the man that he would take a break from scratch-offs this week, but his hands already gripped the bills in his pocket. He sighed, handed him a twenty, and took the bag.

He walked home, stopping to slip the scratch-offs into the center console in his car. He stepped out of the car, looked around to see if anyone saw him. There was no one around. He let out the breath he had been holding in.

Sarah's parking spot was empty when he walked by it, so he was surprised to find her at home. She was standing outside their door, speaking with a petite woman with white hair. Was it Mrs. Davis, the elderly lady from 8F? As he got closer, he saw the woman was in her twenties but had apparently dyed her hair white on purpose. A glance at the logo on the back of her windbreaker said Catholics Care.

"Thanks so much, Mrs. Sortino." The volunteer handed Sarah a blue slip of paper.

"God bless."

"Remember to include that with your taxes."

"Thank you."

Sarah started to close the door. Then she saw him and smiled. She opened the door, bowed, and extended her arm, welcoming him like a doorman at a fancy hotel.

The volunteer said hello to him as she walked toward the elevator.

He waved and walked into his home.

At least, he thought it was his home, although it very much resembled the sparsely furnished space they had seen at the open house with their real estate agent.

The living room had been stripped of most of its furnishings. The sectional couch and television remained, as did the dining room table and most of the chairs. But all the pillows, throw blankets, vases, and other decor that Sarah had curated for them over the past four years were gone, including that awful orange blanket.

She handed him the tax receipt with a curtsy and a giggle.

He ran around the apartment, twitching at the absence of yet another piece of furniture or appliance. How much had it all cost? How many hours of shopping? How many vehicles did it take the charity volunteers to carry everything out? He imagined they would have needed a pickup truck just for the throw pillows.

His body went rigid. He looked out the window at the harbor, hoping that the water would make him calmer.

It worked. He unclenched everything and turned back to Sarah. "Don't you think this is a little crazy?"

"You know what's crazy? How much money I spent on all of this to begin with." Sarah looked around at the room and shook her head. "You know, I bet I could make a career out of this."

"Out of what?"

"Stripping away people's frivolous trappings in search of a purer lifestyle. Marie Kondo is a fricking genius."

"In other words, you did the exact opposite of what you've been doing for your entire career?"

"Yup." She collapsed into a fit of laughter.

Then he remembered the empty parking space. "Sarah, where's your car? Did you donate that, too?"

"Yes."

"Oh my God."

"Nah, I'm kidding. It's at the body shop." She slapped her palm to her forehead.

"What now?"

"I forgot to tell them about the clothes!"

"What about what clothes?"

"Our clothes are next." She ran out of the room toward their bedroom.

"Leave my clothes alone, please."

His pants. Hanging in the closet, with his ticket tucked in a pocket. Their future hanging on a plastic hanger.

"Stay out of my pants, Sarah." He heard muffled laughter

come from the depths of the closet.

Larry ran to the bedroom. She rummaged around in her closet. He flung open the door to his own closet. He lunged for the pants, reaching in the pocket. The plastic pouch was there, nestled into the silky fold of the pocket. He cursed at himself and swore never to get separated from the damn ticket again.

Sarah stood beside him. "You have so many T-shirts. Would you be willing to—hey, what's that?"

She was staring at the plastic holder in his hand.

"An old baseball card." It shocked him how the lie rolled off his tongue.

"Ooh. Is it a rookie?"

His heart thumped in his chest. "Uh, no."

"That's too bad." She sounded disappointed, even though she had never shown anything more than a mild interest in sports. "You could have sold it. An entire village in Central America could eat for a year on a Joe DiMaggio rookie card." She shrugged. "I read it on the internet."

He tucked the ticket in his pocket. "Have you thought more about a divorce?" Ugh. He had hoped to be slicker about it, but the words popped out of his mouth.

"Yes." She walked back to her closet. There were still clothes on the rods, but there were far fewer than there had been in the past. She touched some of the shirts, then turned to Larry. "It breaks my heart that you hate me."

"I don't hate you, Sarah." He meant it. He sure didn't like her right now, but wasn't that natural given the circumstances?

"Nope, nope, nope. Don't deny it, Larry Sortino. You hate me." Her chin sank into her chest with a pout. But then she perked up with a bright smile. "This means I have my work cut out for myself. I must win you back and prove to you that I am still the woman you once loved."

"I don't want you to go to any trouble."

"I sense your reluctance, and I understand I've driven you to that, too. I've damaged our marriage, but I don't believe it's wrecked completely." She selected two of her shirts, one at a time, then gave up. She pushed a bunch of hangers together, tore them off the rod, and tossed the pile of clothes onto the bed.

"Sure, there are a few dings in our sacred union." Now she was attacking her shoe collection, throwing one designer pair after the other out of the closet. Forget selling baseball cards to end world hunger. She could do it by selling her shoes.

"But there's nothing that can't be popped back out and buffed over, good as new. Like the car. Did you know how easy it will be to fix it? The nice man at the body shop told me how he takes this huge magnet and sucks out the dent."

Larry set his jaw. "You're comparing our sacred union to a fender bender?"

"Yes, don't you see?"

"Not even a little bit."

"Everything goes back to that day with me and Dougie in the accident. I don't know what the crushing of metal has to do with a spiritual awakening, but here I am. And here you are. We are in a marriage that is half asunder."

She leapt onto the bed, landing on the pile of clothes and shoes on all fours.

"Larry, don't put this marriage asunder."

"Oh, I don't take any credit for asundering this marriage."

She sank down farther into the pile. "Fair enough." She closed her eyes and breathed.

Was she doing yoga? Meditating? For a moment, she tilted her hips and tossed her head. She opened her eyes wide and focused on him.

"I wanted to be with you the other night after the brewery." She was crawling across the bed to him. "I think you did, too."

Despite everything, there was a familiar stirring within him. He clenched his jaw. Yes, he did want to make love to her the other night. But did he now?

It would be so easy.

He looked down at her hands, fingers splayed on the bed

with chipped pink polish on her nails. An image of Monica's lacquered nails flashed across his brain.

Sarah sprang from the bed and wrapped herself around him.

Well, this was awkward.

He unhooked her arms from around his neck, and she slid off the bed onto the floor, onto another pile of clothes. "I'm going to take a shower," he said.

She mumbled something into her pile of clothes. It sounded like, "I deserve this."

He turned the water up full blast, hoping to drown out the nonsense of his day.

Chapter 17

The next morning, he skipped his bowl of cereal and went to Varma's Convenience Store for a breakfast sandwich. The steel shutter was pulled halfway down. Two customers stood outside, fidgeting.

"What's going on?"

Shrugs from both.

He bent down and looked through the window. The lights were on. A pair of legs he assumed to be Natasha's dad. Odd.

Then, Natasha's face popped into view, startling him.

"Hey, Larry." Her voice was muffled by the steel and glass.

"Isn't it a school day?" He regretted his response. It made him feel ancient.

She made a motion with her hand, and then said something he couldn't hear.

"What?"

"I'm on winter break. Can you please come around to the back door?"

If it weren't 8:30 on a weekday morning and if there weren't a growing line of customers, he might have assumed he was being lured into some sort of unsavory situation. But he didn't peg Natasha or her dad as the type to show up on a wanted poster, so he followed the dirt pathway around to the back of the building.

He entered the store through a door right next to one of the refrigerators. The lights were on and everything was in order, ready for customers.

"What's up?" he asked.

Natasha looked to her father, a blank expression on his face.

"Um, so, about that scratch-off card." She twisted the end of her braid. She seemed nervous. Her father nodded at her. "The one you put in the tip jar the other day."

"Yes, I remember."

"Well, I scratched it. Because you gave it to me, right?"

"Yeah, sure I did."

She tugged on her braid.

Her father's expression was still unreadable.

Well, this was a slow conversation.

"Did you win a little something?"

She looked down at the floor. "Yes."

"That's great! Something good had to come out of dropping a bottle of tea on my shoes. You know, they still smell a bit of mango, but—"

Natasha wrapped her braid around her wrist. Her dad tapped his hand on his counter.

"Oh. Sorry. Um, how much did you win?" He had forgotten that most people were not like him. Most people liked to talk about their lottery winnings.

Silence.

"Is the Larry Sortino Scholarship Fund enough to pay for books your first semester?" He forced a laugh.

More silence.

He looked around the empty store.

"Well, do you mind if I get one of those breakfast

sandwiches?"

"You can take all the breakfast sandwiches you want," she said.

"Why?"

"She won the grand prize," her father blurted out.

"You mean we won the grand prize." Natasha shot her father a look.

"Who did what now?" Larry said.

Natasha walked over to him. There it was, in her trembling outstretched hand—a Made in the Shade scratch-off card that revealed all three beach umbrellas.

"Are you sure?" His voice echoed in his ears, like he was on a public address system at a ballpark.

Out of the many terrible stories that Jordan and Irving had shared about lottery winners, there was one he found hilarious. This guy thought he won the big prize, so he quit his job and told his boss in no uncertain terms where to go and what to do there. But then the boss pointed out to him that he misunderstood the rules, and it turned out he'd won fifty dollars, not five hundred thousand. The video went viral, and the guy lost his job.

But Larry had read the rules and regulations of Made in the Shade at least once a week for the past decade or so. He'd lost count of how many near misses he had when two of the three umbrellas were revealed. He knew what a winning card should look like.

He touched his chest, felt the lanyard was still there. The lanyard that was worth millions more than that stupid, precious game of his that he'd won at last.

Well, he would have won if he hadn't given the damn scratch-off card away.

A laugh caught in his throat and he gagged. Then, with his hand on his chest, like he was pledging allegiance to the New York State Gaming Commission, he passed out in the snack aisle. The last thing he heard was Natasha's dad saying, "Oh shit, there goes the chips."

He came to a moment later. He turned his neck first to the left, then to the right. He heard a loud crunch that startled him at first. Dear God, had he broken his neck? No, the sound came from the now-flattened family-sized bag of tortilla chips under his head.

"The defibrillator is ready," he heard Natasha say. "Help me open his shirt so I can get to his chest."

The lanyard.

"No thank you." Larry sprang to his feet and came face to face with Natasha holding defibrillator pads. Her father was armed with a fire extinguisher, of all things. "I am not having a heart attack, nor am I about to burst into flames."

Both father and daughter took a step back.

"Are you sure you're okay?" She looked disappointed that her CPR skills were not needed.

"I'm fine. I mean, come on, this is a big deal." Larry's voice cracked.

It was his scratch-off. It was his scratch-off. It was his scratch-off.

"But it was your scratch-off," Natasha said.

He knew he liked this girl.

"But he gave it to you," her father said.

"Dad!"

"He put it in the tip jar!"

"Yes, I did. It's your daughter's card. It's, well—"

Father and daughter waited.

He wanted to tell them how many cards he had played over the past fifteen years. To share the memory of that first card his mom played. To confess how much money he had spent on that stupid game.

He wanted to show them his fucking notebook.

"We can split it, maybe?" Natasha said.

"Natasha—" her father said.

"No, that's not what I mean. How do I put this?" Larry looked at the tip jar on the counter and saw a few coins at the bottom of it. "I don't need the money."

"What about your wife?" Natasha said.

"Everyone needs money," Natasha's father said.

What was the father's name? "I'm sorry, I don't know your name."

"John."

"Hi, John. Larry." He pointed to his chest, his fingertip poking the plastic card holder underneath his shirt. "We don't need the money. I don't need to work anymore. It's because—"

He looked out the half-shuttered window and saw more legs waiting in line. For a moment, he marveled at people's patience. Then a foot kicked the door. A muffled expletive. Okay, so not so much patience.

For a moment, he considered showing them his lanyard. He concluded it would be a bad move.

"Can't you just understand that I don't need or want the money?"

"Why?" John asked.

"It's complicated."

"Not good enough."

"Are you trying to muscle me into claiming a prize?"

The man shrugged.

Larry brushed a cheese snack off his pants. He hadn't realized he crushed one of those bags, too. "I'd like Natasha to sign the ticket and claim it."

John sighed. "I'd like her to also. But relatives of store owners aren't supposed to be playing the lottery at the same store."

Larry figured that was a part of the fine print he might have seen but skipped over because it didn't pertain to him.

"What about saying it was a tip? That's what I tried to do." Dumbest move ever.

"That might work, but I'm only seventeen." Natasha chewed her bottom lip.

Damn it. You had to be at least eighteen to play. This lottery business was really beginning to bug him.

An idea came to Larry. "Got it."

John stood up straight. Natasha stopped chewing her lip.

"I need a pen."

John grabbed a pen from behind the counter and handed it to Larry.

"Thanks. That door behind the counter. Is that the office?"

"Yes," said John.

"I assume there's a safe?"

"Of course."

"Good. I'm going to sign the back of the card. That takes care of the winner being a customer and not Natasha."

Tears came to Natasha's eyes.

"No, wait," Larry said. "You're going to put the card in the store safe. You won't be able to claim it because it has my signature on it. When I'm ready to claim it, you'll have to unlock it for me. I'll have a lawyer draw up the papers, and I'll sign the money over to you at the press conference." He spit those last two words out of his mouth. The thing he'd been dreading, and now he'd have to do two of them? No way. He'd have to hit fast forward on his plan.

"So you can't do anything because you don't have the card," said John. "We can't do anything because you signed the card. And Natasha can't do anything until she's eighteen."

"When does that happen?" Larry asked.

Natasha brightened. "April twenty-first."

Oh God. Only two months away. He reached out a hand to steady himself on the rack of potato chips.

Natasha looked at her dad, then back at him. "That makes sense. I think?"

John nodded.

Larry nodded. He felt lightheaded.

"Okay, put the card on the counter."

Natasha placed the card face down on the counter.

Larry leaned over the counter. He signed the back of his

card and wrote his home address. As soon as he lifted the pen, John slid the card off the counter and ran into the back office. A few metallic clicks later and the card was locked away.

John returned with a look of triumph on his face that soon disappeared.

"Wait a minute," John said. "How do we know you'll come back for the ticket?"

"I have every intention of—"

"Dad, he works next door and comes in for a snack every day."

Did Natasha just insinuate he was fat?

"Yes, but he could leave today and get hit by a car on his way home. We're stuck with a card signed by a dead man."

Natasha went back to wrapping her braid around her wrist.

"So could I," she said. "I could cross the street and get hit by a bus."

"Natasha!"

"It's Larry's money to do with as he wants, Dad. Besides, how does he know we're not going to go in there and destroy it?"

"Then no one would get the money," Larry said. "I've already told you I'm okay with not keeping it."

John's mouth fell open.

Natasha's eyes grew wide.

He smiled. "So we're good now, right?"

Larry's stomach emitted a long, loud gurgle. He was hungry. All he came in for this morning was a damn breakfast sandwich.

"Natasha, get the man his breakfast sandwich," John said.

—

Larry finished the sandwich in the time it took him to walk out the back door of the convenience store and around to the front door of Island Tax Prep. He brushed off his hands and opened the door.

"Good morning." He was surprised to find Irving sitting at Jordan's desk.

"Good—" Irving said. He was preoccupied with something on his laptop screen.

"Jordan out sick?"

"He asked if he could take off the morning."

"Hope it's not the flu."

"Nah. He's out there chasing down the news or whatever BS you guys were talking about the other day."

"Oh?" Larry was pleased Jordan took his advice to heart. Maybe mentorship could be a hobby for him in the future. He would call up the alumni office at Wagner College and volunteer to advise some of their accounting students.

"Yeah, he sounded all hyped up when he called," Irving said. "Gotta appreciate his honesty. He could have called out sick."

"Any idea what he's working on?" He was half in his conversation with Irving, half imagining himself as a benefactor of his alma mater. How much money would he have to give for them to put his name on a building? He imagined himself wearing graduation regalia again, this time to accept his honorary doctorate. Yes, he decided that he would make a big donation to Wagner after he claimed his money.

"Sorry, Irv, repeat that?"

"Something about finding out who that bizarro lottery winner is." Irving squinted up at him. "You know, the one who hasn't come forward yet? Man, what's taking them so long?"

The breakfast sandwich started its ascent back up his gullet. He walked past Irving, who was blathering on and on about how if he had won that much money, he would have been on his private yacht by now.

He slipped into the bathroom and closed the door. Panting, he flipped the light switch on, then the switch for the exhaust fan that sounded like an airplane propeller. An obnoxious noise, but one for which he was thankful. In a single retch, he emptied the contents of his stomach into the toilet. He turned on the faucet sink and scooped up some water to rinse his mouth. Then he splashed some water on his face like he'd seen a million characters under duress do in the movies. It didn't help.

He stared at his face in the mirror as if seeing himself for the first time.

This is the face of a millionaire? This is the face of a lucky guy? Too lucky for his own good.

He walked out of the bathroom, certain that his hammering heart was visible through his shirt like in a cartoon.

"Whoa," said Irving. "You okay?"

"Fine, and you?"

"You look like—"

"It's hot in here, isn't it?" Larry walked to the window and opened it, but a flurry of snowflakes came flying through, so he closed it and sat at his desk.

"You're not getting the flu, are you?" Irving's voice was tinged with polite disgust.

"Got my shot. All good." But for a moment, he wished he had the flu. He wanted an excuse to go home and stay in bed for a week.

Did he even need an excuse to go home anymore? He could quit his job. Claim the prize—well, both of them now. Enough with the lottery. He was done playing. But he wasn't ready to claim the money.

Instead, he threw himself into his work that morning. Afternoon came, and still no Jordan.

Irving walked over with his phone in his hand, laughing at something on the screen.

"When's Jordan coming in?" His voice was in a higher octave than normal.

"He called out for the rest of the day."

"Yeah?" He attempted nonchalance.

"He just texted me that he's on to something and he'll see us tomorrow."

"'On to something'?" This wasn't good.

"Yeah, he's hanging out at that convenience store, I think. You know, the one down on Bay Street, where the ticket was sold? He's talking to the salesclerk—"

In his mind's eye, he saw Jordan walking into the Bay Street Mini Mart. He could hear the little bell going *bing bong*. He saw Jordan smiling back at Gaurav's smirk. Jordan slipping Gaurav twenty bucks. Jordan barraging him with questions while he got roped into helping restock the snack aisle in alphabetical order. Sunil wouldn't be there to stop it; he would be outside checking in with his staff at the pump or refilling soap in the car wash.

Or maybe that wasn't how it was going down at all. He didn't always have to think the worst. But he couldn't help it.

Would Jordan do something like that? Friendly, goofy Jordan, who moved back home to care for his ailing mother? Jordan, who he had begun to see as a younger brother—an annoying younger brother, to be sure—on the brink of an exciting career? Larry needed to be a better judge of character. This was getting out of hand.

"But it's tax season." Larry's voice was little more than a whisper.

"Hmm?" said Irving.

"IT'S TAX SEASON."

The staff and clients looked at him in alarm.

He smiled and waved.

"Oh, we're fine," said Irving. "Jeanette's picking up more hours this week. You can, too, if you want."

Larry couldn't talk. His tongue felt like sandpaper.

"Would be awesome if you did," said Irving. "More people will start coming in the door, and with Jordan gallivanting around the Island—"

"Put me down for whatever."

Irving made a note on a sticky note. "Super. Thanks, big guy." Then he walked away.

Big guy? Larry looked down and touched his stomach.

He worked his way through the day in a fog. When his last customer left, he shuffled around some papers on his desk, then shuffled around some more. He was bone tired, like he spent the day digging ditches instead of digging through paperwork.

At a little past 5:30, he gave up. He put on his coat, shot Jordan's empty desk an icy glare, and left. But instead of going home, instead of going to a lawyer, instead of going to a bank or any other thing that would make sense for a lottery winner to do, he went to the local YMCA and signed up for a gym membership.

Chapter 18

The parking lot was full of parents taking their children home from swim and gymnastics lessons. He pulled into a spot toward the back of the lot. The entrance to the facility looked to be a mile away. He'd have no choice but to get in shape if that was how far he'd have to walk to the door every time he came.

The chirpy membership coordinator took him on a tour. He couldn't believe what he was seeing. He knew nothing about the Y beyond the lyrics of the hit song by The Village People. He expected to see an old-school gymnasium with equipment like jump ropes, medicine balls, and the odd pull-up bar. Instead, he saw throngs of people of various ages, all firm and tight like the people who hawked exercise programs on those annoying late-night infomercials. Most of the women wore leggings in such garish shades that he wondered whether he had gone back in the space-time continuum to the '80s, when his mother had dressed up in a leotard and leg warmers and went as Jane Fonda for Halloween one year.

After he signed up for a membership, he walked over to

the easiest-looking machine—the recumbent exercise bike. It was exercise, but he was still sitting, which appealed to him. He got on, plugged in headphones, punched a few buttons on the flat-screen television attached to the bike. He tuned in to some cooking show where the woman kept adding butter to the recipe. It made him hungry and grossed out all at once.

He switched the channel to a sitcom with a laugh track that made the jokes seem funnier than they were. After he had pedaled for twenty minutes, he tapped a button on the machine. The computer console informed him his calorie burn was equivalent to a stick of gum. But he had stirred up some endorphins and felt good, so he decided to stick it out a bit longer. He attempted some stomach crunches on the exercise mat next, but after a few he gave up and just lay there.

A beautiful pair of Spandex-covered legs walked into his line of vision.

"I can see you're working really hard," the legs said. His eyes traveled up the legs to the rest of Monica. She, too, was wearing some crazy pair of leggings and a hoodie that matched. But somehow, she pulled it off.

"Hey, what's going on?" He pulled himself up. He didn't think the Y was her style. He imagined she would have been enrolled in one of those expensive classes involving graceful ballet moves. Or that she had a corner of her basement set aside for gym equipment and had the personal trainer come to her instead. But then he remembered her saying something about being appointed to the board of the Y.

"Just finished with my trainer. God, my butt's killing me."

It was a heroic act of self-control not to look at her butt.

"You just signed up?"

"Yeah."

"If you want to meet my trainer, I can arrange an introduction."

She looked at her watch. "Speaking of introductions, do you want to meet Sammy?"

"Oh, I'm not ready for personal training."

"Sammy's my son." She smiled.

He hopped up and followed her. They walked past a cycling class where the speakers blasted Led Zeppelin. Hmm. Maybe he would give cardio another try.

They walked down a hallway to a door marked CHILD CARE. Delighted squeals emerged from behind it. She pushed open the door to reveal what looked like a kindergarten classroom. About a dozen kids swarmed the space, which was full of blocks in every size imaginable. The manager on duty looked so young that she might have still needed a babysitter of her own.

A dark-haired little boy propelled himself at Monica. "You're back!"

She scooped him into her arms and hugged him. "Yes, I am. And I'd like you to meet someone." She bent down to put him on the floor and gestured at Larry.

"Sammy. This is my friend from college, Larry."

He didn't know what to do, so he extended his hand like he always did when he met someone new. He felt like an idiot for greeting a six-year-old in such a way, but to his surprise, the little guy took his hand with a firm grip.

"Mom can bench press me. What do you lift?"

He looked around and spotted a small toy dump truck. "I could handle that, I think."

Sammy giggled.

"Get your coat. It's time to go home," Monica said.

"Okay, be right back." He bounced away from them as if he were on an invisible pogo stick.

Monica laughed at her son's energy. "Do you ever wonder?"

"No."

She looked at him.

"Sorry. Wonder what?"

"What it would be like to be a kid again."

"Oh, I was never a kid. Just a mini accountant."

They both laughed.

Then he yawned. "I'm beat. Must have been those six crunches I did." He looked at her. "See you soon?"

"Are you planning to become a gym rat, or do you mean lunch?"

"Both, I guess." He was impressed that he sounded so calm. He looked down to find Sammy poking him in the stomach and laughing.

What the hell?

"You think that's funny?" He bent down and flipped Sammy over.

Sammy giggled.

"See you guys," Larry said.

When he walked away, he sensed Monica was looking at him. He looked over his shoulder.

She dropped her eyes and tickled Sammy.

He smiled and kept walking.

—

That night, he woke up in a cold sweat, gasping for air. He didn't have nightmares often, but when he did, he was rattled by the horrible images.

Out of habit, he reached over to touch Sarah. She was indeed there in bed with him, curled up in a tight ball on her side of the king bed. He readjusted the sheets and gave her back her half and even a little extra of the duvet. He pounded a fist into his pillow and lowered his head back down. He stared out into the darkness, trying to make sense of the visions that invaded his mind.

What he remembered of the dream wasn't much to go on, no large-scale narrative that he could roll over in his brain and pick apart until it made sense. His mother was simply staring at him and shaking her head in disapproval.

In the dream, Diane Sortino was coiffed and made up like she was whenever she went to a sales team meeting or hosted a skin care party at someone's house. Sarah sat next to her, also made up. She, too, was shaking her head, but with a playful smirk. Monica stood next to them. She had no makeup on at all. She looked tired and seemed impatient. She was biting her unpolished and ragged nails and looking at Larry. There was nothing scary about the dream per se, but he didn't understand what it meant, which was the frightening part.

He closed his eyes. He too was very tired. He would think about this later. He nodded off. Moments later, his eyes popped open, the trio of disappointed women playing on a loop inside his head.

He assumed that, had his mother still been alive, she would have been happy for his win. But the dream made him remember, yet again, that he hadn't earned the lottery money, not one penny of it. His mother had always been proud of him when he was out there working hard for his paycheck. The lottery, now that was a different story. The lottery was just a game.

All this time, this had been the excuse he'd given himself for the scratch-offs. They were just games, though there was some minimal labor involved in uncovering the prize. Carpal tunnel syndrome was a known risk for scratch-off players. There was no inherent physical danger in buying a lottery ticket with the numbers already printed on it, though. All you had to do was put the ticket under a magnet on the fridge for safekeeping until the winning numbers were announced. He hadn't even done that part right. He clenched his toes and fingers tight when he remembered the debacle with the garbage. How very close he had been to losing the ticket.

Might losing the ticket have been a good thing?

He shook his head. But the image of the garbage, stinky and sticky in the hidden pail, kept coming back. An inner voice taunted him: You didn't earn this. You don't deserve this.

His mother deserved every penny of alimony from his father, though. Larry Sortino, Sr. left them one chilly autumn day with a refrigerator full of food. "I'm sorry" was scribbled on the back of the store receipt that he left on the counter under the fruit bowl, which was also full, though not with the apples Larry preferred. How terrifying it must have been for her to be abandoned, a single mother. Still, after a while, she'd stopped cashing his checks. Diane Sortino supported them both on her own. They had a good life. A home that was cool in the summertime and warm in the wintertime. Enough food on the table that she had to take him to the husky section in the boys' clothing department at the start of each school year. Maybe his mother sat up at night coloring in her own sketch of their house, dreaming of when she could pay it all off. Was that sort of thing genetic? He hoped there was some excuse for him being as weird as he was about money.

Hardworking people, like those who made groundbreaking discoveries after years spent in a lab, they deserved to be rich. Someone who picked random numbers—even under the duress of a snarky convenient store clerk—deserved shitty lavender cupcakes, not five hundred and seventy-five million dollars. Dumb luck, plain and simple.

News reporters would pry into his private life, want to know how he would spend it all, how he'd continued to work a nine-to-five job while sitting on a fortune. He hoped that someone, anyone out there would understand his motives. Perhaps someone would think he was a stand-up guy for continuing to work, a good move in an uncertain economy. No, that last part wouldn't fly. Not now, when Larry's net worth resembled the gross national product of a small country. It wouldn't have been this way if he'd kept to his damn scratch-offs. He would have still been a regular guy with a regular life.

But all that was over now.

Chapter 19

The YMCA closed at ten o'clock. For the past two weeks, Larry had been going every night to make his half-hearted attempt at a workout. He preferred the late hours because all the group fitness classes were over by then and the pool was closed, so he could avoid the crowds. Aside from a few late-night lifters in the weight room grunting between reps, the place was a ghost town. Which was fine by him. He was in no mood to talk.

One night, he was strolling on the treadmill as he watched one of the flat-screen televisions mounted above the wall. He had forgotten his earbuds in the car, so he had to rely on the captions to make sense of the local all-news station that was on. A staff member's voice intoned over the speaker that the gym would be closing in thirty minutes.

He took a frigid sip of the strawberry smoothie Monica had recommended. It was good, but he was perplexed at how anything so sweet could be good for you. He punched a few buttons on the console and started to walk-jog. That was when he saw a huge dollar sign superimposed with a question mark over a silhouette of the map of Staten Island. He had no need for sound to know what it meant.

"The New York State Gaming Commission still has not heard from the lucky Staten Islander who won big over a month ago," the caption read.

He stumbled but managed to grab onto the side rails to steady himself. He continued to read the captions.

"Of course, the ticket holder has a full year to claim the prize. Still, the folks at the New York State Gaming Commission are a bit surprised that the winner hasn't come forward yet."

Blah, blah, blah. He punched a button on the treadmill to speed up the belt. He began to jog faster. Could aggravation make you more athletic? He was about to find out.

A lottery official came on the screen.

"I understand not wanting to let a million people know. But if it were me, I'd have already bought a one-way ticket to a tropical island somewhere." The official chuckled along with the reporter on the scene, her microphone bobbing in his face.

Ah yes, it was all so hilarious.

Sweat poured off his face. When had this become a real workout? He pressed his palms onto the metal sensors that measured his heart rate. A number flashed, and it began to increase rapidly.

The newscaster came back on. Larry tried to read his lips but gave up and waited for the captions to catch up.

"This is the largest jackpot ever to be won by a single winner. With such a large sum, the winner can, of course, expect to leap into the highest tax bracket."

He broke into a flat-out sprint.

"Even so, after taxes, the winner takes home a cool three hundred and fifty-five million dollars."

Shit. That was more than a million below the figure he had calculated. Damn IRS.

"That poor winner." The newscaster's snark was evident even with the closed captioning.

He gritted his teeth and kept running.

The newscaster turned in his chair and mouthed words to the person sitting at the desk next to him.

He wiped the sweat out of his eyes and waited for the captions to catch up.

"With us tonight is Mike Graham, a financial advisor who specializes in working with clients who have won or inherited large sums of money. Mike, good to have you with us."

Larry held his finger on the button to slow the treadmill back down to a walk. His heart thundered in his ears. Maybe the captioning was a good thing. He wouldn't have been able to hear them speak with the way he was panting.

"Tell us," the captions read, "what advice do you give clients who have become overnight millionaires?" The reporter's mouth was out of sync, and the news looked like a poorly dubbed foreign film.

He strained his neck toward the screen. He wished he could read lips. They looked like marionettes talking.

At last, more captions slid onto the screen.

"Well, before they even claim the prize, the first thing they absolutely need to do is—"

The television screen turned black. He stared, bewildered. The belt screeched to a halt. The power had been cut off.

Bastards. Was this the way they kicked members out of the gym at the end of the night? He looked at his watch. Still a full twenty-five minutes to go before closing time.

He was confused, sweaty, and a bit lightheaded. He took another sip of his strawberry smoothie.

Then a shrill voice behind him. "Oh. My. Gawd."

He spun around and spotted a teenager in neon floral pants and a purple sports bra, holding on to a power cord.

"I needed to charge my phone," she said. "I didn't know all that was hooked up to this outlet."

He gave her the iciest stare his overheated self could muster.

"Please plug it back in."

"My phone?" She looked at the heavy cord in her hand, the one trailing from the huge surge protector that Larry's treadmill and the bank of televisions had been connected to.

For a split second, he admired the audacity this young person had to unplug anything just so she could juice up her phone.

"Oh, right." She giggled, then plugged the cord in.

The logo of the television's brand lit up the screen. The cable would take a minute to reboot itself. He would miss the rest of the newscast.

He stormed over to a group of stationary bikes that were in front of another TV screen that was on. He searched for the remote, found it on the seat of one of the bikes, and started jabbing at buttons. At last, he found the news station again, but it was too late.

"Thanks, Mike," the anchor said. "That new loophole will certainly help protect lottery winners. Now I know what to do when I win the big jackpot next time."

The two men chuckled. Since when did everyone think they were stand-up comedians?

"Next up, a new addition to the exotic plant life at the Staten Island Zoo."

He jabbed at the power button.

"What loophole?" he muttered to himself.

Or perhaps he'd shouted it. Yes, he had. Crazy Cell Phone Girl stared at him in horror, grabbed her water bottle, and ran for the locker room.

He downed the rest of his smoothie and swiped at his mouth with the back of his hand. He needed something much stronger than protein powder and almond milk, for God's sake. For half a second, he missed having Dougie as a friend. It would have been so easy to meet him at the brewery. To have a couple of pints and relax. He dropped his head to his chest. Those days were gone.

It was time to go home. He walked out to his car, one of the few that remained in the lot. He saw a dark figure move by the rear passenger door.

Someone was trying to break into his car.

"Hey! You!" He dashed toward the car. An adrenaline rush had taken over.

The guy pulled out a pocketknife. "Whatever money you got, dude. Hand it over."

Larry froze. He had nothing on him. His wallet was in his gym bag, which was in the trunk.

"Give it to me. Now!"

He pointed at his trunk. He felt like an idiot. "My stuff is in there."

"Dumb move. There have been break-ins around here. You should be more careful."

"What?"

The knife flew out of his hand and clattered to the asphalt. The guy whimpered and cradled his bleeding hand.

Without thinking, Larry grabbed the knife and pointed it at the thief as if it were a gun, or maybe a magic wand. Wrong weapon on all accounts. What an idiot. He was never good at fighting, even in video games.

The guy cried out again and doubled over in pain. This time, Larry saw a slender Spandex leg flutter into view.

It was Monica. And she had just drop-kicked the perp.

"Lady, you shouldn't have done that."

She answered the would-be thief with a sidekick to his midsection, then sat on his stomach and smacked him in the head when he tried to get up.

The thief groaned.

"Call 911," she said. She was so calm.

Larry, on the other hand, fumbled with his key fob. "My phone is in the car."

"Use mine." She tossed her phone to him. He glimpsed Sammy's smiling face on the home screen as he tapped in the number and waited for the dispatcher to pick up.

"911, what's your emergency?"

"YMCA on Broadway. Parking lot. Caught someone breaking into my car."

He gave her the phone back. "Why do I get the feeling you've done that before?"

"We've practiced it in kickboxing class. Wait'll I tell them it works."

Five minutes later, the whimpering thief was in the back of a police cruiser.

Monica waved to the cop behind the wheel. "See you next month at the Policeman's Ball, Officer Battaglia."

Larry snorted.

"What?" she said.

"Nothing."

"Look, I don't know if you usually leave a lot of stuff in your car, but I wouldn't do it anymore."

"No, I just left my work clothes and my gym bag in there. All the other lockers were taken earlier." He rubbed his neck where the lanyard chafed him.

But there was no lanyard chafing him now.

Holy mother of God.

He remembered taking it off for a moment in the locker room. No one was around, so he'd taken it to change his clothes, tucking it into one of his pant pockets to keep out of sight for a moment. There were no lockers available, so he decided to keep his bag in his locked trunk instead. He'd figured it would be okay there for his workout this one time.

But he forgot to put the lanyard back on.

He flung open the trunk and practically dove in.

"Larry, it's okay. You said yourself it's only clothes."

He emerged, breathless, with the pair of slacks he wore earlier. He thrust his hand into the pocket. He found the ticket and fell to his knees. "Thank God, thank God, thank God."

He had given away a few million dollars this morning to a girl he barely knew. He would not mess up with his own money, even if it meant stapling the ticket to his chest this time.

She tiptoed over to him and placed a hand on his shoulder. He was focused on his deep breathing exercises, so he didn't even react to the fact that she was touching him.

"I'm going to assume those are designer pants that have you lying prostrate in the parking lot at the Y."

He let out his breath with a soft whistle. He couldn't take it anymore.

"Monica, there's something I have to tell you." He took the lanyard and ran his hands over the plastic pouch. He tore open the stapled side of the plastic and pulled the ticket out. He hadn't touched the actual ticket in weeks, not since the day he found out he won.

He passed the ticket back to her.

"Larry, just tell me."

She took the ticket and turned on her phone's flashlight so she could read it.

The *Advance* had taken to printing the numbers each day in the hopes of jogging the memory of the winner. He knew she scoured the paper every day to see if there were any photos of her, so he was sure she had seen them.

"Are those? Those aren't. HOLY SHIT, IS THAT BONUS NUMBER TWENTY-SEVEN?"

She screamed. And he did too, letting everything out that he'd been holding on to for weeks.

Chapter 20

About a half-hour later, they were sitting in a booth at the Queen's Court Diner. A busboy brought over glasses of ice water.

"God bless late-night diners, huh?" Larry said. "Gotta love New York City."

Monica pressed one of the glasses to her forehead. Her hand trembled. She raised the glass to her lips and downed the icy water in a couple of gulps. She sputtered and took a deep breath, as if she had popped up from a swim in the ocean.

"Hey, hey, easy, you'll get a brain freeze," he said.

A server named Demetrius arrived to take their order.

He was hungry but wasn't ready to undo his twenty minutes on the treadmill. Was that progress in his healthy mindset? Perhaps he might be a jock after all. Maybe one day he would actually run a 10K. Or even a marathon. He could pay an Olympic gold medalist to train him.

Screw it. For now, he needed a plain toasted bagel and a glass of orange juice. Loads of carbs and sugar.

"Mrs. Rossi? What would you like?" Demetrius asked.

Larry rubbed his forehead. Everyone knew her. Everyone.

She studied her place mat, a simple paper rectangle that featured advertisements of local businesses. He knew that those businesses paid a ton to be included on the place mat. Sarah once had asked him about whether she should advertise her interior design services on the place mat, and he'd talked her out of it. It was the digital age, he'd reminded her. Everyone was on social media. But the way Monica was perusing the ads right now, he wondered if he'd given Sarah the wrong advice.

Demetrius waited. Larry reached over and tapped her hand that was on the table. Her hands were very soft. She must have had a budget just for moisturizer.

"Hey. You okay?"

Monica's head shot up, a puzzled look on her face. "Whatever happened to those place mats with the pictures of cocktails and their recipes?" she asked Demetrius. "Do you remember them?"

"You're old enough to remember them? We kept some of them in the back for posterity. Should I get you one?"

"No, I'd like you to bring me one of every drink that's on it."

Demetrius guffawed. "Good one, Mrs. Rossi." He waited for her order.

"Tea and Greek yogurt with fruit. Please."

He wrote it down and left, still chuckling.

She looked at Larry and shook her head. She tucked her hair behind her ears. "Do you understand this entire island is practically sinking with anticipation over who won this damn lottery? And here you are."

"Here I am. No big deal at all."

She leaned in. "Oh, it's a big fucking deal."

They burst into nervous laughter.

"I know. I'm still trying to get this all through my thick skull."

"So you carry your ticket around your neck until you do?"

"Don't chicks dig guys with jewelry?"

"A safety deposit box never occurred to you?"

"No way."

"Why not?"

"Ever see that movie where the bad guys blow up the safety deposit boxes?"

"Fair enough. I hope you have a lawyer or a financial advisor. A good one."

"I've heard good things about this Mike Graham guy, as seen on TV." He was glad he remembered the guy's name. He would have to call him if he couldn't find anyone else.

She tapped her polished fingernails on the table.

The server appeared with their food.

Larry began eating as soon as his plate hit the table.

Monica took her spoon and poked at her yogurt. "But I thought you hated the lottery. You hate all kinds of gambling. Right?" Her sculpted eyebrows furrowed. Maybe she was trying to come up with a snippet of a conversation they had back in college about the perils of gambling. He wished she didn't have to work so hard to remember their time together.

He took a big bite of his bagel. It was so good. New York bagels were the best. If he moved to a tropical island with his winnings, he would have a dozen shipped to him on a private jet whenever he wanted. No, he would have the water shipped in from New York—that's what made the dough so tasty. Maybe he would open a deli on the beach.

He wiped the thought from his mind. He couldn't think about such frivolous things right now.

She ate a spoonful of yogurt. "Let me guess. All this time, you've been one of those guys that spend fifty bucks a week just to win a couple dollars on the stupid scratch-off tickets?"

He twitched.

Demetrius brought more water. They waited for him to fill their glasses and walk away before they spoke again.

"You need to get yourself a lawyer and claim that thing."

"And have every charity in the Tri-state area come knock on my door?"

She dropped her eyes.

"I'm sorry," he said.

They ate in silence.

"Let me see it again," she said.

He wiped his hands several times, then took the ticket out of his pocket. He had put it back in the pouch, but because the staples were undone, he cradled it in his palm. She looked at it and giggled.

"You're like a little kid," he said. Little kid. Sammy. "Oh God, we left Sammy at the Y."

"No, no, he's fine. He's sleeping over at my mother's house tonight." Her blue eyes scanned the ticket. Her impossibly long eyelashes cast shadows on her cheeks. He knew a little bit about mascara from his mother and Sarah, but he concluded that Monica's feathery eyelashes did not occur in nature.

"And Max?"

"Away on business." She stared at the ticket, mesmerized. "This is huge." She grabbed his other hand.

His hand twitched. His thumb grazed over the back of her hand. He glanced up at Monica. She was looking at him now.

In that moment, Larry only cared that he was happy. Soon he would be very rich, but right now, he was very happy.

So happy that even when he saw Jordan standing outside the window of their booth, grinning at them, Larry smiled back and waved. So did Monica.

He released Monica's hand.

"How many people know?" she asked.

It occurred to him in that moment that he had told Monica before Sarah. He swallowed the last bit of his bagel, which now tasted dry.

"Um, not many." His face burned. He took a sip of water. The icy liquid soothed the shame he felt and brought him back to the real issue: Someone else knew about the ticket. What now?

Monica squealed and grabbed his hand again.

Something bright flickered near their booth. They turned to

look.

A light shone right into his face. Monica gasped, then dropped his hand.

When he could see again, there was Jordan next to their booth, smiling. He was with two other men, one with a rather large camera and the other holding a microphone on a boom.

Jordan was saying something. Words were coming out of his grinning mouth. The vocal exercises were paying off. His New York accent was all but gone. He had achieved the ultimate goal of a television newscaster: to sound like you came from nowhere. Jordan's words were clear yet so confusing. Larry needed captions to make sense of them, like he had back at the gym.

How long had Jordan been on his tail?

Those perfectly formed words continued to pour from his mouth with astonishing fluidity, but Larry couldn't hear any of them. His heartbeat thumped in his ears.

At last, his brain caught up to what Jordan was saying.

"After weeks of speculation about the identity and the sanity of the elusive lottery winner, I have tracked the winner down to, of all places, the Queen's Court Diner."

"Turn the camera off, please." But the guy didn't turn off the camera. Perhaps he didn't hear Larry.

"Many of you know Larry Sortino as your neighborhood tax man."

"Jordan." A little louder, but still not loud enough.

"Dedicated to his clients, as evidenced by this late-night appointment."

Monica ran her fingers through her hair and pressed her lips together.

"The moment you've been waiting for, Staten Island. Here is the winner of the Power Payday jackpot. A multimillionaire is in our midst. Ladies and gentlemen, I give you Larry Sortino and his good friend, Monica Rossi."

Larry swallowed with great trouble.

Monica waved at the camera like she was at one of her charity functions.

Someone from the next booth came over to give him a high five. Someone else slapped him on the back. Patrons left their chairs and booths to gawk at the real, live rich person in their midst.

Jordan leaned over the table. "Oh boy, and he's got the ticket with him. Can we get a close-up on this?"

The camera guy stepped forward and zoomed in on the numbers.

"That's it." Larry stood up from the booth. He punched Jordan right in the mouth.

Jordan fell on his ass. The momentum of his breaking-news energy propelled him backward across the polished floor.

"Keep rolling, keep rolling." Jordan skidded to a stop at the feet of Demetrius, who was carrying a tray of fresh baklava.

Demetrius had better reflexes than Jordan. He stayed upright, the tray remained full. People at a nearby table applauded. It was well deserved. The man looked like a Greek statue: Demetrius, god of dessert.

Jordan managed to sit up. He leaned back on a booth. The occupants of the booth stared down at him with a mixture of interest and disgust.

Larry shoved the ticket deep inside the pocket of his running pants. He accepted a glass of ice water from Monica and poured it over his aching hand. Punching someone was awful. Too much pain, not enough payoff. Jordan was stunned only for a few seconds.

The cameraman and boom operator swiveled back and forth from the booth to Jordan, still on the floor.

"Guys, get me in a close-up," Jordan called to them. The pair brought the camera closer and dangled the microphone over his head. Jordan smiled into the camera lens.

"There you have it, folks. Larry Sortino is the lucky winner of the lottery jackpot." He saluted the camera. "This is Jordan

Brunner, reporting for whatever news station I want."

The diner owner stormed over. He frowned at Jordan, who was still grinning into the camera. Once he saw that no one was hurt, just stupid, the owner gestured to Monica and Larry to follow him. He escorted them through the kitchen and out the door to the parking lot on the side of the building.

Larry fumbled for his wallet.

The owner opened the door and held up his hand. "Do not worry, sir," he said in his musical Greek accent. "You can pay another time." He leaned in. "I hear that you are good for it." The door slammed behind them on the man's loud laugh.

"Crap, shit, damn, hell, fuck." There were five steps that led to the parking lot from the door. Larry dropped a fresh four-letter word on each one as he trotted down them with Monica. Good thing they were both in their gym clothes. Who knew if Monica would be able to move as fast in heels?

Larry jumped off the last step and ran to his car, aware of the fact that the camera crew and Jordan would be coming out the front of the restaurant. He wanted to be long gone before they did.

"Larry, wait!"

He skidded to a halt. Oops. Where were his manners? First, he didn't pay for his bill, and now he had forgotten to say goodbye to Monica.

She walked toward him slowly. Too slowly. He eyed the front door of the restaurant and willed her to speed things up.

"I'm sorry. I'll talk to you soon. I have to, this—"

Finally, she touched his arm.

"Hey. It's going to be okay."

His mouth opened several times to say something, but nothing came out. His hand started to twitch, so he ran it through his hair to cover up the motion.

"Really, Larry. You've got this."

Did he? What was "this" anyway? "This" seemed to him like everything and nothing all at once.

She gave him a gentle shove. "Breathe."

He closed his eyes and breathed in. He opened them, and there was Monica in his arms.

She touched his face. "Breathe."

He obeyed.

She kissed him.

He had never had a second chance at a first kiss with someone before.

It wasn't much of a chance. She broke away with a gasp and pushed him back before he could respond. "Go."

"Monica, I—"

"We'll talk more soon. You need a lawyer. Maybe a few. I know some good ones."

She was all business once again, but he could detect even in the dark that her cheeks were flushed.

"Hey, Monica—"

"Go." She slammed the door to her car. And she was off, wheels screeching as she drove out of the lot.

He got into his car. Going home didn't seem like an option. He kept driving, his left hand on the wheel and his right hand resting on the center console until the throbbing subsided.

He sped along an empty Forest Avenue. He turned on Clove Road, then Hylan Boulevard. He took it the entire stretch from Grasmere to Tottenville. Nothing was recognizable to him. He hadn't been on the South Shore in years. Never had a need to be. The way it was on Staten Island, you could stick to a few neighborhoods for the purposes of daily life, traveling through other neighborhoods on the way to Brooklyn or New Jersey. It's no wonder he and Monica hadn't seen each other all these years. It was possible to move to another part of Staten Island and never be seen or heard from again, at least not outside of social media.

He reached the end of Hylan Boulevard, made a U-turn, then headed home. But instead of going straight back to his condo, he drove to Howard Avenue and made the slow ascent up the hill to Wagner College. He parked at the edge of Sutter Oval and got out. The icy grass crunched beneath his feet.

He stared out at the lawn that led up to the entrance of Main Hall. He had spent countless hours here, hanging out with friends in between classes. He could almost feel the sunshine warm the top of his head, hear the chatter among his friends. What did they talk about back then? What made them happy? What troubled them? For a moment, he saw all his friends there on the Oval, young and happy.

There was something on the Oval that he didn't remember from his school days. He walked the path around it to a small monument. He squinted at it in the dark. The words on the etched metal plate read: In Memoriam, 9/11/01.

Three columns of names were listed below. Some had graduated many years before him. Five graduated his year. He recognized one of the names: Mark Barnard. A brawny guy from his biology class who played on the baseball team. Larry would often see him in the cafeteria with two trays, both piled high with food. Now he was gone.

He shivered and sniffled as he drew his coat tighter around him. The words on the monument grew blurry. He swiped at his eyes with the back of his coat sleeve and walked back to his car, the taste of Monica's kiss still on his lips.

Part 3

March

Chapter 21

Jordan's video made the homepage of the *Staten Island Advance* website the next morning. It was uploaded as of 8 a.m., but the little ticker showed ten thousand views already by the time Larry saw it around 8:30.

He refreshed the screen. The number climbed to fifteen thousand. He refreshed again and it was already up to twenty thousand.

He texted Irving that he was sick, even though he knew his boss probably already knew the truth.

It used to be that in the case of a public scandal, one could run down to the newsstand, buy up all the newspapers, then discard them in an abandoned trash barrel or perhaps set a discreet bonfire. A poor man's investment in damage control. In the digital age, however, unless you knew how to bring down the internet, the news would find a way out. Fast.

He burrowed under the covers and watched the video again. It was worse than he had imagined. Far worse. Wasn't it supposed to be the opposite—something was never as bad as you envisioned it to be?

There he was with Monica. They were smiling at each other like lovers enjoying a tryst. She was clutching his hand. Of course, it was the lottery ticket that had her all excited. People wouldn't jump to conclusions, right?

Then again, she did kiss him when they left the restaurant.

He touched the pause button on the video to get a closer look. He tried to see it through the eyes of a nosy Staten Islander, who would have forwarded the video to a dozen friends and family before breakfast. He groaned. He knew what it looked like. He knew what people would think. They would be wrong.

Or would they?

He replayed the video, then paused it.

In the freeze frame, he looked like he was about to sneeze. She was gorgeous and glowing. He looked at her dark curls and the absurd length of her eyelashes. Who knows how long it would be before he saw those blue eyes again? After this debacle, they would both have to lay low for a while.

He refreshed the site. It was up to thirty thousand views. Given that half a million people lived on Staten Island, perhaps that wasn't so bad.

But it got worse. He saw that another new video had been uploaded to the site.

He touched the play button and flinched when he saw who came onto the screen.

It was Sarah.

The crack down the middle of his phone screen made it a bit difficult to see. It looked like she was inside a warehouse. She was dressed in a Wagner College sweatshirt and leggings and was surrounded by other people who were filling boxes with cans of food.

"He never mentioned a thing, that sneaky Pete," she said. "Granted, he did get home very late last night, and I was already asleep. But when I saw the news today, I was so pleased for him."

"For him? Isn't it your prize as well?" The voice that came

from off camera didn't sound like Jordan, but then again, he didn't know Jordan like he thought he did.

"Oh, we're getting a divorce."

"Say what?" Yup, it was Jordan.

"Yes, we are getting a divorce." Sarah stared into the camera. "I destroyed our marriage by having an affair with my husband's best friend."

He wanted to stay there under the covers for the rest of his life. But he couldn't take his eyes off Sarah. She was both dazzling and humble. For a very weird moment, he was proud of his wife. Or his soon-to-be ex-wife. His breath caught in his chest.

"But Mrs. Sortino, wouldn't you receive half the prize in the divorce proceedings?"

Sarah shook her head with gusto.

"I broke our marital vows. I don't deserve any of the prize money. What I did is my cross to bear." A flash of sadness across her face, then she flashed a glorious smile at the camera. "But I do hope that Larry will honor my request to donate a portion of the money to Project Fresh Start." She shouted the last part and threw up her arms, as if she were a model on a game show.

The other volunteers ran to the camera and cheered as if they were on the big screen at Yankee Stadium.

Fuckity fuck fuck. Why'd she say that? Now that damn charity and a dozen others were sure to be calling him to make good on Sarah's pledge.

The camera cut to Monica in a crisp navy business suit. She wore dark sunglasses and clutched her purse in both hands. Her high heels clacked on the sidewalk. "I'm thrilled for Larry. He and I are old friends. Yes, we dated in college, but that was a lifetime ago. Who can even remember?"

His jaw clenched as Monica got into her car and slammed the door, the camera still fixed on her. Couldn't blame the camera guy. She was beautiful. "I am happily married," she said, her voice muffled by the closed window. Then she drove away.

Irving was next on the screen. "We're all in a state of shock here at Island Tax Prep. To learn first that Larry Sortino, the best member of our team, is indeed the winner."

A smile flickered across Larry's lips.

"And then that our other team member, Jordan Brunner, was the one to rat him out."

An annoyed grunt from off camera.

"Oh. Sorry. I mean, that Jordan Brunner, um, produced the, uh, investigative report."

He threw his phone across the room. It crashed against the wall. He winced. He would need a new phone for sure now.

He flipped over on his stomach and shouted a stream of profanities into his pillow. He shouted until he almost asphyxiated himself in the eight-hundred thread count pillowcase. He kicked his legs and thrashed his arms. The exertion made him gasp for air and brought tears to his eyes.

He needed to talk to someone. But he'd run out of people to talk to. Where had all his friends gone? He had the same phone number since he first got his cell phone, and yet the only calls he received these days were from telemarketers.

A former coworker at Parker & Rosenthal once bragged that he had five best men at his wedding because he had five best friends. Larry thought that was an oxymoron. How could you have five of anything that was "best"?

Although he could buy the best of everything, right now he'd settle for even one friend who was just okay.

—

He woke with a gasp when the front door slammed.

Sarah? Was she alone or was she with a charity volunteer? Was there anything left to donate? There were very few pieces of furniture left and almost all the décor was packed up in small, tidy boxes.

He jumped out of bed and peered around the bedroom door.

He tiptoed out to the kitchen. Sarah was in there with a bag of groceries.

"Oh." A hand fluttered up to her heart in surprise when she saw him. She almost dropped the paper sack. "Hey, Lah." She smiled.

He couldn't believe it. She was happy to see him.

He settled on, "Morning."

She beamed at him. "Are you okay, Mr. Millionaire?"

"I'm fine."

He didn't feel fine. He worried that she was upset by the video and the insinuation that there was something between him and Monica.

"Look, I'm sorry that I didn't tell you about what happened. I was going to. I panicked."

"I knew something was up with you. You've been acting so strange lately."

He couldn't think of anything to say in response.

"And I'm so sorry you got laid off."

His hand twitched three times. It was a moot point that he'd been laid off by his former employer, but his body hadn't got the message.

"I'm so happy you didn't donate the bed yet."

"Now there's an idea!" She saw the expression on his face. "Kidding."

"Well, then, if you don't mind. I'm so tired."

"I was on my way out again anyway."

He had wanted nothing more than to be alone for a bit. But now, he didn't want her to leave. He wanted to talk to her. About what, he didn't know. There was so much to say, so much to ask her. He had no idea where to begin.

"Is there anything for breakfast?"

She smiled and walked into the kitchen, giving him a "follow me" wave.

She took out a loaf of the cinnamon bread that he liked and popped two slices into the toaster. She poured him a cup of coffee and handed him the container of milk. She had long ago given up on how he took his coffee. She tried, but she always added too much or too little milk for his taste. She used to get upset about it, believed it a failure on her part as a loving wife that she couldn't complete the simple task of preparing her husband's coffee in the morning.

They stood in silence as they watched the bread brown in the toaster.

"Is it true what you said on the news?" he said.

"What part?"

"We're getting a divorce and you don't want any of the money."

She shrugged her shoulders. "Haven't I caused you enough grief?" She sounded like the old Sarah, back before the high-priced interior design clients came calling and buying candles and throw pillows was a competitive sport.

She smiled, but her eyes had grown shiny. "I haven't seen you happy in a long time. Who am I to keep you from the one person that may change that?"

"Sorry, what did you say?" His shoulders tensed up.

"I said, who am I to keep you from the one thing that may change that?"

His shoulders relaxed.

The toast was ready. She took it out of the toaster, put it on a plate, and handed it to him with a flourish. She pointed to the knife and tub of butter on the counter. She had given up on how much butter he liked on his toast, too.

He reached for the plate.

The doorbell rang. "No!" He thrust an arm in front of her to hold her back, as if they had skidded to a halt in a car. "It could be more reporters."

"Oh, no worries. I told them you hightailed it to a craps table in Atlantic City." She made a little clicking sound with her tongue and cocked a hip to one side. Sarah was adorable, even after all this time.

She walked to the door. He peered around the wall and saw her reach for the doorknob without looking through the peephole. This surprised him. Even in a secure building like theirs with retired cops on duty at the front desk, she insisted that they still uphold a certain level of security. This meant squinting for a full minute through the tiny peephole that was always blocked by some elaborate door hanging she would swap out each season. Their door was bare right now, which would have made it easier for her to see who was there, but she didn't bother to check. It was clear that her new lease on life included having a lot more trust in her fellow man.

He ducked back into the kitchen. All he wanted was to eat his damn toast and go back to bed. He took a huge bite of a slice before he went out to see who the visitor was.

It was Max Rossi.

"Don't say nothin', don't touch nothin'."

At first, he assumed Max was talking to Sarah. But then he saw Sammy next to him.

"Here." Max offered Sammy his hand to hold.

Sammy shrugged and took his father's hand. They walked through the door upon a sweeping gesture by Sarah. "Jehovah's Witnesses. Welcome!"

Max raised an eyebrow.

"C'mon, Sarah, you know who I am."

"Larry!" Sammy ran over to give him a high five.

"Hi, Sammy." He sighed. "Hello, Max."

Sarah stared at Max, then broke into laughter when she recognized her old classmate.

"My goodness. Max!" She ushered them into the living room. "It's been a while since our Consumer Behavior class, right? Would you like some water or...water?"

"No, thanks." Max's eyes scanned the apartment. "Did yous just move in?"

Yous. Larry bit the inside of his mouth.

Sarah laughed like his question was the funniest joke she

had ever heard, then headed into the kitchen. She gave Larry a look as if to say, "What now?"

Max walked up to him, hand extended. They shook hands.

"I came to congratulate you and your wife on your recent good fortune."

"You saw the video."

"I think everyone on Staten Island did." *Stah Nyland.*

The two men nodded at each other.

"I'm sorry, that story was a bit misleading." He decided damage control was the way to go, and he was going as fast as he could.

"So yous didn't win the money?"

"Oh no, I, um, we won the money." God, this was awkward. "I meant, I'm not having an affair with Monica, even though that might be how it looked." Larry started to laugh, then stopped. If there was anything worse than thinking your wife was having an affair, he figured it would be someone laughing at the idea of your wife being desirable enough for an affair. He didn't want to offend Max Rossi either way.

He also regretted using the word "affair." It sounded so strange, from another time. The word evoked an image of two lovers in formal dress, swirling around a crowded ballroom as an orchestra played and people jabbed their fingers in accusation. It made him dizzy.

"Save your breath. Monica would never cheat on me." His tone was a perfect cross between "No worries, brother" and "Fuck you."

Larry was relieved, then disappointed. He tried hard not to let his face betray him, but the smug look on Max's face told him he'd failed.

"Well, I'm glad we cleared that up."

"She can't even buy gum without telling me."

"But that video..."

"No harm, no foul. Anyhoo, I didn't come here to talk women." Max adjusted his collar. "Sammy, go sit and be still."

Both men looked over at Sammy, who had already found a small cardboard shipping box to sit on and was flipping through one of Sarah's home and garden magazines. He looked at his father and nodded.

"Kids," Max said, with a snort.

"Not to be rude, but people usually find me at my office." Larry wanted this social call to be over. Besides, if Monica wasn't the reason for him to be here, then what was it?

"Like I said, I stopped by to offer my congratulations to an old friend."

The two men nodded again.

"Which charity?" asked Larry.

"'Scuse me?"

"You want me to donate to one of your many, um, charities."

"Charities, schmarities. Don't get me wrong. I love philanthropy. Keeps Uncle Sammy away." Max chuckled. It sounded like he was coughing up phlegm. Larry didn't know which was worse, that disgusting laugh or the way he said *philantruppy*. "But this isn't a charity call. I want you to join me in opening a second country club."

"Really?"

"Picture it. Not one but two Olympic-size pools. Lazy river. Big wading pool for the kiddies as well. Racquetball, basketball, pretty much whatever kinda balls you want. Hot tubs. Cabanas as far as the eye can see. I found this sweet piece of property out on Long Island." *Lawn Guyland.*

"Sounds great."

"I've got the deposit, but I need a partner."

"What do you need a partner for if you've got the deposit?"

"Well, as it turns out, money doesn't get you everything like it used to."

"I don't understand."

"Let me cut to the chase. Banks don't like it when they get paid in small bills."

"Don't you write them a check?"

Max smiled. "I make most of my money through my clubs."

"I thought you had just the one country club?" He cringed. "Sorry, that came out wrong."

"Nah, man, it's all good! You're stepping into your filthy rich life." Max snorted. "Yes, Larry, I own just the *one* country club." He leaned in. "But I own several gentlemen's clubs, too. And when you want to get funding for something that's more, uh, family-friendly like a country club, banks don't take kindly to your prior business reputation."

"Got it."

"Larry, may I use your bathroom?" Sammy's sweet voice floated across the room.

"Sammy, don't whine."

"Of course. Right down the hallway, kiddo."

Sammy trotted away. Max's cell phone rang.

"'Scuse me." He swiped at the screen. "Rossi." His voice got deeper. "Hellooo."

Larry turned away, embarrassed to be in his own home. He wondered where Sarah had gone off to. He thought of his toast growing cold on the counter.

"I can't, I'm in a meeting," said Max, his tone both seductive and nauseating. "I'll see you in an hour."

He assumed Max was talking to Monica.

"I'll drop my son off at home and then I'll be there."

Something flared inside him, but all he could do was glare at Max.

Max ended his call.

Larry tried to reassemble his facial features into a more neutral position. But it was difficult to be a gracious host when Max Rossi was the guest.

Max must have noticed the change in his expression. "You look confused 'bout something." *Sumpen.*

He knew what he meant. Max knew he knew what he meant.

Larry took the bait.

"Was that Monica?"

Max shrugged.

"Ladies are like stock portfolios. I like to diversify."

Larry blinked, like a dummy. "Right."

"But not many people know that." His tone was playful, but Max wasn't playing.

"Of course."

"Look, Larry. I'm a god on this island. I'm Santa Claus, the Easter Bunny, and the Tooth Fairy all rolled up into one."

Larry mouthed "Tooth Fairy." He nodded like he understood what the hell Max was talking about.

"I'm a nice guy." Max made quotation mark motions using his middle fingers. "Stupid pictures in the newspaper, like the one of you and my wife?" He waved his hand and puffed air out of his fat, ugly lips. "Monica don't have the balls to pull off anything like that."

Larry swallowed hard and looked down the hall for Sammy. Good. He was still in the bathroom.

Max was on a roll. "You or anyone else, for that matter, can't make me look bad. I don't look bad." He jabbed a fat thumb at his chest with each word. "I donate a lot of money to a lot of people every year."

Sammy returned.

"Tuck your shirt in," Max said to his son. Sammy and Larry both looked down to see that the boy's shirt was already tucked in.

Sarah came from wherever she'd been hiding. She held a bowl of fruit. "Fruit?"

Larry took a small bunch of grapes and rolled them around in the palm of his hand.

"No thanks, I'm doing keto," said Max.

She looked down in disappointment, then brightened. "Hey, I think it's great that you've done so much for the Genie's Lamp Foundation."

"Remind me?" Max looked pleased.

"The one that sends kids to theater camp."

"Right. They're good people over there."

Sarah smiled, then turned and left the room.

"See what I mean?" Max cocked his head in Sarah's direction.

Larry saw what he meant. It all made sense, and he hated all of it.

"But hey, it's time to get going," Max said.

Sammy got up from his box and waved at Larry.

"Oh, and before I forget," Max said.

Here it is. Larry braced himself.

"I don't want you to think I'm always all money, money, money." He took a step closer and leaned in. "I'd like you to do my taxes for me."

"I would have figured you already had an accountant on staff, Max."

"Yeah, I have someone who does my taxes, but I need for someone to *do* my taxes, *capeesh*?" Max raised his eyebrows.

Larry was ashamed to share the same ancestral homeland as this troll.

"Yeah, no, in that case I don't *do* taxes."

"That's a shame." Max leaned in even closer. Larry feared he would pass out from cologne fumes. The guy stank the same way he had back in college.

"As I said before, I'm fine with those pictures in the news. That's because I know Monica would never go for a guy like you."

He bent down and whispered in Sammy's ear. The young boy went back to sit on the box. Larry popped a grape in his mouth. He was so hungry.

"I mean, I know you fucked her in college and all."

He choked on the grape.

"We, uh, we—" He could feel the grape stuck in his gullet. "We never—"

Max shrugged. "Ah, whatever yous did. So what. Even Monica said that was all a million years ago."

Larry's right hand twitched. He reached behind his back,

scratching at an itch that wasn't there. As he did, the lanyard tightened around his neck. He could probably take it off now. The jig was up.

"But you're right," said Max. "Other people who don't know the truth might misconstrue. You know what happens when people misconstrue?"

"They get whacked?"

Max threw back his head and snorted. He sounded like a penguin. "Nah, no one's gonna get whacked. But they could get their feelings hurt."

"Right."

"So as much as that stupid video was nothing, I don't want to see any more stupid videos of you with my wife. *Capeesh*?"

"I understand."

"Now, about my taxes."

"No."

"Come on."

"I don't know what kind of business you do, and I don't want to know."

"Not sure what you're insinuating, pal, but what I do isn't anything different from what any other smart entrepreneur does. Believe me, I give Uncle Sam more than his fair share." He cleared his throat. "See, I kinda hoped you'd see what goes on behind the scenes of my empire and want in on some of the action yourself."

Empire? Was this guy serious? Larry bit his lip to smother a laugh.

"I appreciate you looking out for me, but I'm all good the way things are."

"The door's still open. When you're ready to do some business, put some of that moolah to good use, you give me a call. But in the meantime, you need to relax, pal. You're too tense." Max reached into his jacket pocket and pulled out one of those foam stress balls and tossed it at Larry. It bounced off Larry's forehead and onto the floor.

"Let's go, Sammy," Max said.

"Bye, Larry."

They left. He closed the door, picked up the stress ball, then went into the kitchen. The toast was ice cold, but he devoured it anyway. He chewed while he squeezed the stress ball. Chew, squeeze, chew, squeeze.

Max was right about one thing: He did need to relax. The stupid stress ball was helping.

He looked down at the foam ball and saw it wasn't a ball at all. It was in the shape of a high-heeled shoe. "The Rendezvous" was printed on it in pink script letters.

Max gave him a glimpse into his empire, all right.

And it gave Larry an idea. A very good idea.

Chapter 22

The next morning, after he had finished his cup of coffee, he stayed out on the terrace a few minutes longer to practice his deep breathing exercises. He swapped out one of the yoga mantras he learned in class with one of his own. *I will not kill Jordan. I will not kill Jordan. I will not kill Jordan.*

Larry did not condone violence. Apart from that one punch, he had never been in a fight, and he didn't enjoy violent movies or television shows. He disliked boxing and wasn't a fan of martial arts or wrestling, much to the chagrin of Dougie, who got ringside seats for WrestleMania every year. Sure, Larry knew all that was fake, but he didn't like any of it. For him to contemplate any type of ill will toward Jordan was a step in a direction he'd never thought he'd go.

He had never needed to be in a fight. He was tall and stocky enough that no one was ever dumb enough to pick on him. He had no practice, no experience to draw on other than that one punch he threw at Jordan, which he landed out of dumb luck. But oh man, he was ready for a fight now. It was as if he had held off on fighting for his entire life so he could have the energy for this one.

Around eleven, he showered and got dressed for work. He took the elevator down to the lobby. Head bowed, he flicked his coat collar up and made it past the doorman and several neighbors without being recognized.

He decided to take his car to the office this time. He wasn't being lazy, but he needed to make a quick getaway, if necessary. He pulled into a spot in front of the office door. He threw the SUV into park and glared at the storefronts of both Varma's Convenience Store and Island Tax Prep. The office had a sign in the window that read, "It's ten days until the tax deadline. Do you know where your forms are?"

He cut the engine and got out of the car. He decided to go to the convenience store first to pick up a box of doughnuts for the office.

The door opened and the bell tinkled. At first, he didn't see Natasha or John. He glanced over at the newspaper rack, half expecting to see his own face staring out at him from the headlines. But then he remembered that the newspaper must have already hit the stands before his video hit the internet. Thank goodness for small favors.

He heard a cackle.

"Here he is, the luckiest man in the world!"

Oh no.

John came out of the back office. He was recording Larry on his phone.

"Wave to the camera, Lucky Larry."

God, this dance again? He waved to the camera.

"Natasha, get in there with him. Hug him. This man turns everything he touches to gold."

"Da-ad." But Natasha came out from behind the counter and hugged Larry.

"Now I understand why you don't need the money," she whispered.

"Do you ever go to school anymore?" he whispered back. She laughed and said it was St. Joseph's Day, so she had off.

"You, too, can be a big winner, when you shop at Varma's Convenience Store," John said.

Two of the other employees jumped out of nowhere to stand behind Larry and Natasha, waving at the camera.

"And cut," said John, pressing a button on the phone. "Okay, Natasha, post this to social media. Make it get a virus."

"Da-ad, you mean make it go viral."

"Whatever. Just get it out there. Welcome back, my friend!" He pounded Larry on the back. "So, my friend. I understand everything now, you lucky son of a bitch. I was planning to give you free snacks for life, but now I charge you triple." He let out a booming laugh.

Natasha shook her head and smiled.

Larry waved and left the store, forgetting about the doughnuts.

Nothing to do now but go to the office.

The door opened and everyone looked up, staff and clients alike. Even the water cooler man turned around with interest.

They all burst into thunderous applause.

He forced his lips into a smile. But he wasn't there to be congratulated. Stone-faced, he stalked over to Jordan's desk, but he wasn't there.

There weren't many places to hide in the office of Island Tax Prep. Even if there had been, he didn't need to search for long. Jeanette stood up and pointed to the kitchen. He nodded his thanks.

Sure enough, Jordan was in the kitchen, eating a powdered doughnut while he waited for a fresh pot of coffee to finish percolating.

He heard him come in and turned around with a powdery grin. "No hard feelings, right?"

The doughnut flew up in a sugary cloud as he dragged Jordan to the sink. He shoved Jordan's head under the tap. He would have preferred to use the water cooler, but there was no way that big fat head was fitting under the spigot. He turned on the faucet full blast.

"Man, that's cold!"

"The water or whatcha did, Jordan?" Larry's New York accent was in full flight. He didn't care. He wasn't the one trying to make a career on television.

"Touché," said Jordan.

Larry pulled the retractable hose from the sink and blasted him in the face with a spray of water.

"I'm not a good swimmer." Jordan sputtered. He squeezed his eyes shut, then opened one to squint at Larry.

Irving and the staff came over to the breakroom entrance. If Irving was upset that one of his employees was attempting to waterboard another, he didn't let on.

Larry nodded to his coworkers, then returned to the matter at hand.

"What did I ever do to you, Jordan?"

"Let me collect my thoughts."

Larry adjusted his grip on the hose trigger. "Collect them fast."

Jordan slicked his brown curly mop of hair back off his damp forehead.

Larry fired a warning shot from the hose at the ceiling above Jordan.

The water dripped down onto the head of Staten Island's new star reporter. "You told me to chase a story," he said.

"You were chasing after me! You couldn't have asked first?"

"You wouldn't have let me do it." His voice came out high-pitched and whiny, like a child's.

Larry took a closer look at him. Jordan was young. He could have been his teen dad.

"You encouraged me to search out the news." Jordan's voice was stronger now, but he kept his eyes down.

Larry shot him again with the hose. "Wrong answer. Try

again."

"Please stop. I'll catch pneumonia."

"You son of a bitch."

"I didn't know you were the winner."

"No one did!"

"Come on, dude." The whine was back. "It's a good story. Local and hard-hitting."

"But it's my story! It's my business!"

"It's not personal. It's journalism."

"You're right. You're a professional now. Good work."

"Really? You mean it?"

"WHAT DO YOU THINK?"

They all flinched. Irving looked at Jordan and shook his head.

Jeanette clucked her tongue in time with her knitting needles. The sound was both soothing and judgmental.

"At first you had my sympathy," Larry said. "You moved back home to help your sick mother—"

"Sick mother?" said Jeanette.

Jordan's eyes grew wide.

Larry looked at Jeanette. "He moved back to take care of his mother." He looked at Jordan. "Right?"

"I never said that."

"His mother had her eyes lasered when she was up from Florida." She rolled her eyes. "Now he lives at his mom's place rent-free while she's at her condo in Boca Raton. He waters her plants for her." She looked around at her coworkers and waved her needles. "You think I can't hear you all when I'm knitting?"

Jordan's shoulders drooped.

"Oh, I see. You don't have a mother who's an invalid. My mistake. Fine, well, the second thing I'm going to do is sue you for invasion of privacy. I'll go for everything you've got."

Jordan crinkled his brow. "Wait, what's the first thing?"

"I'm glad you asked."

He took a couple of steps closer to Jordan. He looked over

his shoulder to his audience. "Hey, guys, thanks for stopping by. I got it from here."

One by one, Irving and his coworkers returned to their desks. The water delivery guy man saluted. Jeanette brandished a knitting needle at Jordan.

When the last person was gone, he turned back to Jordan. "I'll reconsider my lawsuit in exchange for a favor."

"A favor?" Jordan sounded nervous, but Larry could tell he was intrigued.

"Yes. A favor. But I promise, you'll like it." He pulled the foam stress ball from The Rendezvous out of his pocket and handed it to Jordan. "Here's another hard-hitting story for your résumé."

Chapter 23

Larry didn't consider himself to be an intimidating man. After all, his weapon of choice was a retractable sink hose. However, Gaurav's reaction when he walked into the convenience store later that day told him that yes, he could be an imposing figure when he put his mind to it.

The damn bell tinkled as he walked in. If this were a Western, he would have taken a pistol and shot it off the wall. But he had no pistol, and there was nothing to shoot at—it was just a computerized bell with a hidden speaker. So, while his entrance didn't quite pack the dramatic punch he had hoped for, it was gratifying to see the coward choke on his iced tea and run behind the counter. He pretended to help his father at the cash register. Sunil smiled and patted him on the back, then went into the office behind the counter.

There were half a dozen customers in line. Larry didn't care. He had all the time in the world. He walked into the snack aisle and browsed the snacks, arranged in alphabetical order. Gaurav had been hard at work. He wanted to fill his arms with cellophane candies and cookies and fling them around. Or, at the very least, take all the M candies and switch them with the S candies. That would show the bastard.

He had a fistful of marshmallow bars, but he decided not to go through with it. He kept one for himself though, then grabbed a package of cookies, another chocolate bar, and a package of strawberry licorice. He had been hitting it pretty hard at the gym lately, so he figured it was okay to indulge in some empty calories.

He got in line, staring Gaurav down as he checked out each customer.

The last customer in front of him, a man clad in paint-splattered work pants and a dingy hooded sweatshirt, stepped forward with a bill in his hand. He left a strong scent of nicotine in his wake. Larry assumed he was going to buy a pack of cigarettes, but no. In a gruff voice, the man asked for ten number nine scratch-offs. Gaurav reached for the roll and counted them off. The stinky customer dropped the bill on the counter, took the scratch-off cards, and walked out.

At last, there was no one else in the store. Gaurav looked panicked, like a cornered animal.

Sunil emerged from the office. "Mr. Larry! Hooray!"

Gaurav swung himself over the counter and knocked over the cupcakes—green in honor of St. Patrick's Day. Sunil's mouth dropped open.

Gaurav was fast, but Larry beat the little shit to the door. He spread his arms out to block Gaurav, who slammed into him and smashed his head into his collarbone. Larry winced.

"Hello, Gaurav." The disdain in his voice was colder than the frosty machine that whirred nearby.

"Excuse me, sir, I have to check on the soap in the car wash."

"Sir, my ass. I'm sure there's plenty." He grabbed Gaurav by the hood on his sweatshirt and hauled him back toward the counter, his sneakers squeaking on the vinyl tiles.

Sunil hadn't budged. Larry figured he had to have expected

something like this would happen to his obnoxious son at some point.

"Can we use your office, Sunil?"

The man nodded and opened the door behind the counter.

Once they were all in the office, Larry loosened his grip on Gaurav. He gave him a slight push, and Gaurav collapsed into an armchair.

Larry looked around for a moment in awe. The office, no more than six feet by six feet in size, was bright and modern. The furniture was sleek and minimal. A huge computer screen sat on the desk. The comfortable armchair in which Gaurav sat panting was situated on a rug that even Sarah would have approved of. This tiny little closet of an office looked like an executive suite in one of the slick start-ups that he had audited back in the day. At first, he imagined that Sunil and Gaurav had gone shopping with the incentive money they won from the lottery, but he got the feeling that this stylish office had always been here, tucked away behind the day-to-day madness at the store.

"Sunil, I have a score to settle with your son."

Sunil sighed. He looked like he was on the parent side of a parent-teacher conference that was about to go south.

Gaurav stared down at his jeans and began to pick at a small hole in the knee. Larry wondered if they had been ripped by accident or if he bought them that way. He had never subscribed to the fashion trend of clothing that was already damaged. In high school and college, he would buy clothes and simply hope for the worst to comply with the look of the season.

He took a deep breath. "As you know, I won the lottery last month." It felt so odd to say those words. He had only said them once before to Monica. *I won the lottery.* Well, and everyone that night at the brewery. But that didn't count.

His mind whirred. His left hand twitched. He placed his hand on his chest, over the ticket, and took a deep breath. Then another.

"Mr. Larry, should I call for an ambulance?" Sunil said.

He took a third cleansing breath and shook his head. "Can you tell me what the store does to track lottery ticket sales?"

Sunil gestured to his son. "You'll have to ask Gaurav. He handles all of that."

Larry should have known that Gaurav did a lot more than just stand at the register or alphabetize the snack and candy aisle all day. The young man did have an MBA in finance, so it was clear he had a head for numbers. It made perfect sense that Sunil would entrust his son with a major part of the store's budget: the lottery receipts.

Gaurav got up and walked over to the large computer monitor on the desk. He sat down, tapped a few keys, and brought up on the screen one of the most breathtaking spreadsheets Larry had ever seen. It stirred in him a feeling that was almost sexual in nature. "I would kill to do your taxes." His voice was husky.

Gaurav laughed, but for once, not in a mean way. He showed him his real work behind the scenes at the store, how he kept track of every lottery transaction. Larry might have been the biggest winner the store ever had, but he was by no means the only winner they ever had. The Bay Street Mini Mart sold lottery tickets and scratch-off cards that won something, even if it was just a free ticket, every single day of the week. It was Gaurav's responsibility to account for each of them at day's end. Every dollar coming in and going out had to be recorded. He displayed the massive spreadsheet that he sent to the New York State Gaming Commission each week. No wonder Gaurav had such contempt for him and his scratch-offs. All those stupid little prizes had to be tracked, every free card accounted for. But with Larry's big win, more was required than a column on a spreadsheet. Gaurav had spoken with the Gaming Commission at least a dozen times to ensure that everything was on the up and up with the ticket and the transaction as they waited for the winner to emerge. He had even become friends with one of the lottery officials who worked there.

Larry was mesmerized by all the rows and columns. He felt

lightheaded when he saw the pivot tables.

"Thank you, Gaurav," he said.

The two men shook hands.

"I'm very sorry. The idiot with the camera came and paid me one hundred dollars. What would you do?" Gaurav said.

Larry was impressed at the dollar amount. He hadn't suggested bribing sources to Jordan in the name of journalism, of course. But he liked to think his pep talk led to Jordan's boldness, even if it backfired for him.

"It's okay. Really." And it was okay. Or at least it would be.

But not yet. The edges of his vision began to blur and his knees started to soften. Sunil pushed another chair over and caught him. He sank down into it and closed his eyes. The chair was comfortable. He could drift off to sleep right here. Maybe he could ask Sunil if he could stay here for the night.

Perhaps he did drift off to sleep. He was startled when Sunil cleared his throat.

"Now that everyone knows I've won," Larry said, "I'm going to need your help."

Chapter 24

It took some coaxing, but Larry made Irving understand that he wanted to finish out tax season before he put away his calculator for good. He did, however, ask for a few days off.

He stayed home alone in the near-empty condo. Sarah was out volunteering each day. He wondered what had happened to her interior design clients, but she was up and out so early that he never had the chance to ask her. He considered joining her at the food pantry but cringed at the photo op it would create. He could hear the camera clicks. It made him think of Monica. He went back to chasing every meal with antacids.

One afternoon, Larry turned the ringer off on his phone so he wouldn't be disturbed and fell asleep on the couch while watching a documentary about the royal family. When he woke up, it was early evening. He reached for his phone, now patched together with clear packing tape, and saw a bunch of texts from Sarah. Lately, she'd been texting him from her volunteer gigs at regular intervals with mundane items like the weather forecast, random sports facts, and the odd request to *please bring home*

X from the store, thank you so much!

When her car came back from the body shop, she did decide to donate it to the charity that had that annoying radio jingle. She bought a second-hand bike instead, but the roads were too icy for her to pedal. He wished she would just walk to the store like he did whenever she needed an item or two, but he knew what would happen—she would forget that she didn't have a car, fill up a shopping cart with a gallon of milk, a case of soda, or a three-month supply of paper towels, and then have to lug it all home. She knew it, too, so she asked him to shop for her instead. She would text him a series of emojis to indicate what she needed—chicken, potatoes, assorted fruits and vegetables. He was always surprised by the ever-growing emoji selection. Sometimes she would text a series of photos that didn't make sense to him, so he would text her back for clarification. The other day, she had sent him a line of bubbles followed by a glass. He'd had no clue what it meant. It turned out she wanted a bottle of seltzer.

This time, he was surprised to see there were actual words in the half-dozen texts. But he still didn't understand what in the hell she was getting at. This line of communication might have annoyed him before, but now, complete calm radiated from the top of his head to the tips of his toes. Perhaps the meditation app did work. The last time he could recall feeling like this was when Sarah insisted they go for these expensive massages for his thirty-fifth birthday. That was three years ago. He made a mental note that when he cashed in his ticket, he would make an appointment for another massage. Maybe several.

So, in his Zen state of mind, he decided to call Sarah.

He tapped the button for speakerphone so he didn't have to put his cheek at risk from any shards of glass that poked through the tape. Maybe he would grow a beard to protect himself from his phone. He could always pluck out any gray hairs. Small price to pay for not slicing and dicing his face.

She answered with a whisper on the first ring.

"Where are you?"

"At the hospital."

And just like that, his Zen got zapped.

"What now?"

"I volunteer here now, remember?"

No, he didn't.

"Anyhoo, can you come here? I'd like you to see someone."

"What do you mean?"

"There's a patient here I'd like you to see."

"Sarah, I'm not a doctor."

"I mean to visit, Lah. Sheesh."

He had only ever been a visitor at a hospital. He had never broken any bones, never required any stitches, never had his tonsils or appendix removed. But when his mother was diagnosed with cancer, he drove her to appointments at the hospital twice a week for the better part of a year. During the last few weeks of Diane Sortino's life, when she was admitted for full-time care, he had taken to sleeping in the chair next to her bed.

He ground his teeth as he neared the hospital on Seaview Avenue. He didn't want to use the same visitor parking lot he had used for all the morose visits to his mother, so he turned down the block before the hospital, where there were spots reserved for short-term visitors. It meant a longer walk and perhaps having to deal with one of the wild turkeys who liked to loiter there. The rather unattractive animals—"Ugly like my ass," Dougie would say with fervor—had long since taken up residence in the hospital neighborhood. They were harmless, if a little unsettling, but they would keep their distance, provided people kept theirs. Also, he didn't want to deal with the chatty parking attendant who had worked the booth for the past thirty years and would likely be there for the next thirty.

He found a spot at the end of a long row of cars. Sure enough, as he pulled in, a wild turkey strutted away.

"What's up, Tom?" he said to the turkey. The turkey made a

clucking sound that sounded like an "Eh, can't complain" retort, then turned and ambled down the street.

He was glad to see Sarah in the lobby waiting for him so he could get to the bottom of why he needed to be here.

A warm smile passed over her face. "Thank you for coming." She reached for his hand like she was going to shake it, but instead covered his with both of hers. She guided him toward the elevator. "I'm not sure how much time we have." Her tone was still bright, yet businesslike.

"Visiting hours are until eight, and it's only..."

He clamped his mouth shut, a strange feeling in his stomach. Someone was dying. Who was it?

They stepped onto the elevator. Sarah pressed a button, and it began its slow ascent. His body grew rigid. He should have taken the stairs. He was more than fine with the elevator in their building, but he didn't like being in this slow-moving steel box that carried people who were sick or in pain.

The elevator came to a gentle stop with a ding that struck him as too cheerful. When the doors whooshed open and he saw they were on the oncology floor, everything came rushing back to him. The sights, the sounds, the God-awful odors. It had taken him months after his mother died to erase the memory of that horrendous antiseptic smell. He grew very hot, then in the next second, it was like he had plunged into an ice bath.

He moistened his lips and opened his mouth to say something.

Sarah patted his arm. "I know," she said, her voice devoid of the brightness that was there a moment ago. "I'm sorry. But I think you need to do this." She took his arm and steered him to the left hallway.

He snapped back to the present, to this awful place. "Do this? Do what?"

Someone was dying. But who? And what could he do about it? Why did she insist he come here?

As if in a dream, he walked down the hallway with Sarah, in

the same direction he had gone so many times when his mother was there three years ago. He recognized some familiar faces among the doctors and nurses. He even remembered some of their names.

Sarah stopped at a door. "Here."

Through the glass pane in the door, he saw a single bed on the far side of the room, partially hidden behind a curtain.

He stared at the handwritten name on the card outside the door. He squinted at the letters, then stepped closer. Did he need glasses? No, the letters were in focus, but the name didn't make any sense to him.

The name card read SORTINO, L.

"Sarah." His voice echoed in his ears. "What is this?"

The calmness that he'd enjoyed earlier was a distant memory. In its place was a dark heaviness. Jumbled images of his childhood flashed across his brain, and then they turned to black, angry static, like a broken TV.

"But Mom said he died."

As he said it, he knew that it had been a lie.

He breathed in and let it out with a whistle. Breathwork, as he had learned from his meditation app. But this was not relaxing, not calming or soothing like it was before. Now he was breathing just to keep the oxygen flowing to his brain, which he still wasn't sure was working as it should.

Sarah rubbed his back. "Come on."

They stepped through the door. He was grateful to have her hand on his back. It kept him from toppling over onto the bed or from bumping into any of the equipment that surrounded the hospital bed.

A sickly man laid in the bed, motionless. The heart rate machine blipped. The ventilator hissed.

He stared down at his father.

"How old is he?" Sarah asked.

"Seventy-five. I think." His voice didn't sound or even feel like his own.

He searched the old man's pale, wan face for even a hint of himself. He didn't find any, and he was glad. When he was a kid, he always hated it when people told him he looked just like his mother. Now, he was thrilled. He didn't know what he would have done if he had stared down at this person, this man, his *father* in the throes of death and seen himself.

There were times he couldn't bring himself to look at his own mother toward the end. The cancer had ravaged her body so much that he was afraid the pressure of his gaze would weaken her further. He'd had to force himself to stare into the eyes of the woman who loved him and raised him. When he looked at her, he remembered it all, their wonderful life together, which would soon end. There was one time that he fainted and landed on the large feet of one of the attending physicians. The impression of the good doctor's shoelaces stayed on his cheek for a few hours after the incident.

"How did you know?" He forced himself back into the surreal present.

"Coincidence. This is my first day on this floor. I brought around the snack cart, and here he was."

He felt drunk. He needed to sit down.

Sarah slid a chair over to him, the metal legs scraping the linoleum. They both watched the old man. There was no movement, not even a tremor of an eyelid.

The younger Larry sat, surprised at the effort it took. His muscles ached as if he had finished a hard workout.

A nurse walked in. "Oh, hello." She looked at a machine, her lips tucked into her mouth in a grim scowl that did not fit with her otherwise pleasant face. She made a note of something on a clipboard attached to the foot of the bed. "Are you family?"

Sarah nodded. He opened his mouth, but no words came out. Did he have the right to give an affirmative answer to that question? He had long since given up on any hope of association with this man, yet here he was.

The nurse's face turned solemn. "He's had a rough week. I'm

so glad you were able to make it here." She nodded and left the room.

It was the end. Larry knew it. He stood up again and walked to the side of the bed.

Sarah slipped her hand into his and squeezed. "Say something to him."

He shook his head.

"Forgive him. He's all alone."

Larry was mute. Even though he had long since stopped going to church, he had faith that something was out there, something bigger. He believed in the idea of crossing over into everlasting life. But he wanted no part of this man's crossing over.

His hand twitched and Sarah squeezed it.

He looked at his father. This man, whom he never gave the satisfaction of putting Jr. after any of his signatures. The man who had abandoned them. And for what? A life of nothing. Or so his mother had led him to believe. She was the one who had told him he died. When was it? About ten years ago. He had been at a doctor's appointment and was filling out some paperwork. There was a question about the medical history on his paternal side. He called his mother and asked if she knew anything about her ex-husband's background.

"He was full of shit," she said. "I do know that much. But I heard he's dead now, so that's all we'll ever know, sweetie. I'm sorry, but it changes nothing." She hung up the phone, and he never asked his mother about his father again.

Larry stared down at the man whom he'd presumed was dead. Was "presumed" even the right word? It wasn't like he disappeared after a parasailing accident in the Bermuda Triangle or something. He remembered looking for an obituary, and he couldn't find one. What would there have been to read, anyway? What could a three-paragraph article tell him about the man who had abandoned them?

But Diane Sortino had lied.

Sarah's warm hand in his comforted him more than he expected it would. Someone who walked by the room might have surmised that here was a loving couple, supporting each other during the agonizing wait for someone to move on from this life. Looks could be very deceiving.

He stared down at the near corpse. He wanted to feel something. He begged his body to feel anything. But there was nothing. The anger that had consumed him minutes ago blew away like dust. Now he was empty. Could the lack of any feeling be the same as forgiveness? It would have to do.

As if she could read his mind, Sarah squeezed his hand again.

"I forgive you." He mumbled the words that meant little to him.

"Louder."

"...forgive you."

"Come on, Lah."

"I FORGIVE YOU." He shouted the words into the dying man's face. There could be no misunderstanding now. Sortino the Elder opened his eyes. He looked at Larry, who stared back into eyes like his own. Pools of hazel. Proof of his paternity.

He was no longer mad at his father. He was no longer mad at Dougie, for that matter, either. How could he be? Everyone does what they have to do to get by in this world.

Just then, a man in his late twenties or early thirties came into the room. He carried a small tray of food from the cafeteria. "Hey, Dad, I'm—" He stopped when he saw them. He looked puzzled. "Oh, hello."

Sarah dragged Larry back from the bed.

Did he just call the man "Dad"?

They all stood there, like they were in a play and someone forgot a line.

"I'm the hospital's interior decorator," Sarah said. She adjusted two of the carnations in a vase of flowers on the bedside table. "There. Isn't that better?"

"And I'm the hospital accountant." Larry's voice once again sounded like his own. "There was a problem with the bill for the TV. It's all good now. You have the movie channels free for one week."

Sarah grabbed his arm, and they headed for the door. They ducked out of the way of another nurse heading into the room. They marched down the corridor to the elevator. The floor seemed less crowded than before, or maybe he was intent on not seeing anything or anyone right now. When they made it past the nurses' station, they broke into a run. This time, instead of the elevator, they took the stairs.

His mother lied to him again. His father didn't have an empty life. He went on to live a different one, started a new family. And he certainly hadn't died.

Well, at least not yet.

They flew down the stairs and out the door, almost knocking over a very pregnant woman.

They speed walked through a long hallway leading to the main entrance, dodging patients in wheelchairs and evading a group of well-wishers with huge helium balloons in the shape of a baby pacifier and a bottle. They glided through the revolving door. The cold night air hit them and they ran.

"I'm so sorry, Lah!" His name bounced out of her. "Lah ah ah ah." She sounded breathless, making him wonder if she had given up running altogether. Not that he had any business judging her. He, too, gasped for air, not able to say anything. He willed his legs to keep running, to get away from there.

They reached his car and flung open the doors and jumped in. He started the car and pulled away, then stopped short to let another turkey cross the road.

Chapter 25

At last, he gave in and bought a new phone. The tips of his thumbs throbbed from all the tiny cuts he got from texting. What a stubborn fool he was. It wasn't as if he couldn't afford it.

He went to the cell phone store at the mall, picked out the latest model, and paid for it outright, despite the sales associate's admonitions that they had a low-interest payment plan and an insurance program. He'd waved a bandaged hand to stop the eager associate mid monologue. By the time the credit card statement was due, he'd have his prize money. He could smash and buy a new phone every day for the rest of his life if necessary. Still, he vowed to be much more careful with his new phone this time around.

About ten seconds after his new phone was all set up, a litany of texts from Monica appeared. She shared a bunch of phone contacts with him—attorneys, financial advisors, and the like. It was a good thing he got his new phone when he did, otherwise he would have sliced up his cheeks with all the calls he had to make. And he would have to make them soon. So much for his calendar and his plan to lay low for a while.

His phone blerped a few more times. Damn those factory-set ringtones and alerts. He would need to spend some time scrolling through options like Busy Bee, News Alert, and Happy Hour before he landed on a sound that wasn't an assault on his eardrums.

He looked at his screen and saw a text from Monica that, at last, was not a contact name or a phone number. "Meet me in the parking lot?"

He smiled and texted back. "Which one?"

"This one."

He looked up and saw her across the balcony on the other side of the mall. She put her hand up in a half wave, then tucked a curl behind her ear. She took the escalator down and walked toward the exit.

He put his new phone deep in a pocket and followed her out of the mall.

He stayed about fifty feet behind her in the parking lot. When she got into her car at the end of a long row, he picked up his pace. He walked to the passenger side and got in.

She hit a button, and the door locks whooshed shut. "Did you make any calls?"

"Not yet, I just got my new—"

"Larry, you have to get this thing moving. I know it's not going the way you wanted it to, but the faster you do this, the faster everyone will leave you alone."

"Maybe I don't want to be alone after all." He told her about Sarah. Not everything—he left the whole Dougie debacle out because it was too embarrassing—but he talked just enough about the last dying gasps of his marriage to garner, he hoped, some sympathy. They were on common ground now, two people with spouses they didn't know anymore.

It must have worked. She leaned in, cupped her hand behind his head, and kissed him hard. Their lips mashed together. It would have been smoother had he been prepared.

This was not at all how he envisioned their reunited bliss to be. He had imagined that gentle kind of kiss, where the couple takes a full minute to move their mouths into the same vicinity. Movies, he concluded, were a poor tutorial for romantic overtures. In movies, kisses were either smooth and sexy or goofy and sexy. Sexy was the common denominator. There was nothing sexy about this kiss that he shared with Monica. Kissing her reminded him of those bumbling first kisses he initiated with girls in high school—too fast, too much tongue. In this instance, it wasn't even his tongue that was too much. He had tried to be a gentleman in his response.

This kiss was reminiscent of their first awkward embrace back in college. He decided that he didn't care.

She gasped and pulled away. She dabbed at her mouth, now two dark pink smudges.

Was her gasp necessary? He understood why she did it the first time—her kiss was just a physical manifestation of her excitement for his win. This time, however, she should have known what she was doing and why she was doing it.

He attempted to mimic her embarrassment. He swiped the back of his hand across his mouth. His heart was a rapid, rhythmic thump in his chest. "That was nice," he said.

"I'm sorry."

Not the words someone wanted to hear after a kiss.

But this time, he had no problem looking her right in the eye. "Are you? Because I don't think you are."

"You're right. I'm not."

And when they leaned in to kiss each other again, he almost believed her.

Part 4

April

Chapter 26

As a CPA, Larry had seen fifteen tax seasons come and go. This would be his Sweet Sixteen, as it were. More like Bittersweet Sixteen. He had given up trying to explain to people why he found accounting so fascinating. How he loved the glimpses of people's lives behind the numbers. No, he wasn't ready to let it all go yet.

His attorney had been in communication with the Gaming Commission and set up a timeline for him to claim his prize, but he still wasn't a rich man.

Island Tax Prep would remain open for a few days past the April 15 filing deadline to accommodate frantic late filers. After that, it would close for the rest of the year. Irving would shift back to the home office in Brooklyn until it was time to do it all again starting in January. So, in the days that led up to April 15, he did what he always did: Larry went to work like a normal person. He wanted to cling to any last shred of normalcy for as long as he could.

Irving spit out his sip of coffee when he saw him walk in.

"What are you doing here?"

"Told you I wanted to finish out the season. Plus, I need to file my own taxes while I'm still able to make sense of them."

It was true. Somehow, in all of this, he had pushed Parker & Rosenthal so far out of his head that he almost forgot about his own W-2 form that had sat on his desk for the past two months. He would stay after his last client of the day to file his own tax return.

A young man in a faded black T-shirt with Greek letters emblazoned across the front sat down at his desk with a big smile. He reminded him of the frat boy who had been here last month.

"Didn't I do your taxes already?"

"No, dude, I'm Kevin. That was my fraternity bro, Dave." He laughed like it was the funniest thing in the world. "He recommended you. So here I am."

"He said he would." Larry gave him a genuine smile. He had always appreciated referrals. This would be one of the things he would miss about the working world. Now his referrals came from local charities. He'd pushed so many calls to voicemail in the past week. Nearly a dozen non-profits had gotten his number and were "just calling to introduce" themselves. The director of the Wagner College Foundation wanted to take him to dinner.

"D's a stand-up guy," Kevin said.

"I'm sure he is."

"He told me you hooked him up with a pretty sweet refund. Can you do that for me?"

"Well, we'll see."

And so, the number crunching began. The mellow young taxpayer tried to be polite and look interested in the work, but after a while, he gave up. He pulled his phone out of his pocket and swiped at the screen.

Larry became engrossed in the numbers, so he wasn't paying attention when Kevin the frat boy transformed into Kevin the fan boy.

"Um, excuse me, but..."

"Yes?"

"Dude, is this you?" Kevin held up his phone.

Larry glanced up. The homepage of the *Staten Island Advance*. There was a photo of him with his deer-in-the-headlights look. The headline read, "WINNER OF OUR DISCONTENT."

"Mm hmm."

Kevin slid off his baseball cap and scratched his head. "And you're still working?"

"It's tax season."

"Dude. Come on."

He put his pencil down and looked up at Kevin. The bro part of him seemed to have washed away.

"What's your major?" he asked him.

"Communications."

"Perfect. You'll understand."

"Understand what?"

"I'm sort of sitting on a big announcement."

Kevin's serious look dissolved into laughter.

"Yeah, but dude, with your money, I'd pay someone to sit on that big announcement for me and head to the beach instead."

Larry laughed. It was funny. He got it. He knew everyone would have an opinion on how he should spend his money. He just didn't know that everyone would have the *same* opinion.

"All in good time. But I'd prefer Rome."

"Wherever you want, dude. I wouldn't be anywhere near an office if I was you."

He printed out some papers. He stapled them and turned them around so Kevin could read them. He pointed to a figure.

"This is what you'll get back."

"Noice." Kevin reached out and shook his hand. "It's an honor, dude." He looked solemn, but then he broke out into laughter again. "You totally don't make sense to me, but it's all good."

"You keep up with the local news?"

"I try."

"Ever watch it on TV?"

"Sometimes."

"Watch Channel One tonight. It might make more sense to you then."

—

After the final relieved client left, Larry and Irving sat in the empty office, eating the rest of the doughnut holes he had brought his coworkers for breakfast. He had skipped going to the gym a couple of days and imagined that he was piling back on the pounds with each sugary bite. He didn't care. Soon, everything would change, and not only because he would be able to afford a private chef and a personal trainer.

"What are you going to do now?" Irving asked.

"Not sure." Larry popped a third chocolate donut hole into his mouth. "I'd like to go back to Italy for a bit."

"Nice." Had this been a conversation with Jordan, he would have been compelled to recite a list of things he would do, things he would buy. But with Irving, he could talk in vague terms and it would be enough.

"Hey, you want to go for a beer or something?" Irving asked, which made him wonder what Dougie was up to these days, even after all that had happened. When things settled down, maybe he would reach out to him at some point. But not now. Not for a while.

"Another time, if that's okay. Lawyer's coming tonight."

"The one to claim the prize?"

"No, the one to claim my divorce."

Irving choked on a doughnut hole. Larry pounded him on the back and he recovered.

"Oh. Hey, sorry, guy." Irving clapped him on his shoulder.

"Things happen." He smiled, grateful that he called him "guy" and not "big guy" this time. He'd lost another couple of pounds. He reached for yet another doughnut hole, then reconsidered.

—

He had no idea what to expect with his divorce. Sarah was so amiable lately that he didn't expect anything too awful, of course. But if someone had used the word "smooth" to describe the process with their lawyer, he would have called them a liar. No one's divorce proceedings were smooth. No legal proceedings of any kind were smooth for that matter. But these were strange days indeed. The Sortinos' divorce proceedings were not only smooth, he would say they were downright pleasant.

He hadn't experienced cold feet when they got married. Instead, his doubts came with the divorce. Perhaps amid this lottery craziness, all they needed was some time. Maybe if they took a breather, they'd be okay. Things were moving too quickly, and he didn't feel good about any of it. Granted, he didn't think many people felt good about getting divorced at all, not even those newly minted ex-spouses who were eager to celebrate their freedom. Even they had to work through some serious emotions to feel reborn. Larry and Sarah had somehow skipped all of that. It was a monumental task to commit to marriage in the first place. And now here he was, working up the courage to commit to its dissolution.

Although Monica had provided him with a cadre of legal references for claiming the lottery money, those attorneys dealt with estates, wills, trusts, and the like. He needed a divorce lawyer. Could he consult the attorney he chose for the lottery about his divorce? How gauche would it be if, after discussing when and how he would accept the prize, he made an inquiry along the lines of, "While I have your attention, do you also handle divorces?" or "Please transfer me to your divorce department."

Instead, he went old school. He found an actual phone book at the office, thumbed through it until he got to the legal section, and called the number of the law firm with the largest ad. If the attorney with whom he spoke knew who he was, she didn't let on. Her tone was crisp and professional, though it did have a tinge of someone paying their respects at a funeral.

He figured filing for divorce would take time, would drag out for months. But the attorney shook her head when he asked her about it. "The process moves faster when I have clients as easygoing as you two."

As it turned out, the attorney lived in one of the neighboring buildings and offered to come to the condo to have them sign the paperwork to begin the proceedings. They all sat at the table in the dining room, which looked enormous now that the place was devoid of most of the trappings of their so-called domestic bliss.

"Mrs. Sortino," the attorney began. "By signing this contract, which you asked me to draw up of your own volition, you are renouncing any portion of the lottery money."

"Yes."

"And as I asked you on the phone and will ask you again now, with all due respect, are you insane?"

Sarah smiled and shook her head.

"I mean, you must understand that you are due half of this money. Mr. Sortino has not contested that at all. And, of course, New York State law is on your side as well."

"I am deeply grievous of my former trespasses and feel that I am unworthy of any material aspects from this marriage."

"Except for—" Larry said.

"Except for the condo, which Larry has given me along with an escrow account to cover HOA fees for the next twenty-five years." She bowed her head to him.

The attorney raised an eyebrow at Sarah. "I need both of you to sign and date here."

They signed the papers. The attorney left, mumbling something under her breath. Then Sarah left. She was going on a week-long retreat with her church.

Larry Sortino was alone in his kingdom.

Well, it was Sarah's kingdom now, which was not at all how it was supposed to be.

Chapter 27

At two minutes before 10 p.m., he switched the channel from a documentary on the Swedish Olympic curling team to the local news on Channel One. A commercial for erectile dysfunction medication was on, so he took the opportunity to get a glass of water. He was back on the couch in time to hear the laundry list of all the horrendous side effects of the medication. He wondered what it would take for something not to get approved by the Food and Drug Administration.

The news anchor smiled at the camera. "Good evening. At the top of tonight's newscast is a shocking exposé of one of Staten Island's most prominent business owners and philanthropists. Here is Jordan Brunner, the newest addition to our team of correspondents. Jordan?"

The camera panned to Jordan, whose gelled coif and half-inch layer of pancake makeup made him look like a life-sized Ken doll.

"Thanks, Tom. Strip clubs. Escort services. A high-profile business owner on Staten Island has used revenue from these questionable ventures to fund dozens of charities across the Tri-state area."

A photo of Max Rossi appeared on the screen. Larry shuddered. He took a sip of water. He wished he had picked up some beer on the way home.

"Max Rossi. You know him as the owner of the exclusive Cardinal Crest Country Club, as well as the new luxury hotel and business complex on the North Shore of Staten Island. He and his wife, the former Monica Scotto, are also the benefactors of countless organizations across our borough."

As Jordan spoke, there was a montage of video clips of the Rossis, power couple extraordinaire. There was one of them as they cut the ribbon of the new children's wing at the hospital. Then another of them wearing hard hats and holding shovels at the groundbreaking of their new hotel complex. The last one showed the happy duo standing on a float and waving in the St. Patrick's Day Parade on Forest Avenue. Or rather, Max looked happy. Larry couldn't help but notice that as the videos progressed through time, Monica looked more and more unhappy.

Jordan continued. "Max Rossi donated over a million dollars to charity in the past two years alone. But are his hotel and country club really doing that well?" The kid knew how to work the camera. The part of him that didn't still seethe over the betrayal was proud of Jordan.

The screen cut from Jordan in the studio to an exterior shot of a seedy-looking bar. He saw the inside of a club bathed in garish blinking lights.

"It's long been known that Rossi likes to dabble in other types of business." He leaned into the camera. "And those types of business are definitely booming."

Larry smiled. In the end, Max had gotten his way. Larry might not have done his taxes, but he did do some exploring of his "empire." The guest parking lot at the hotel was half full most days. They were still running ads in the newspaper to attract new members at the country club, whereas a competing country club had a two-year waitlist.

But Max's charitable donations had been increasing year over year. There was only one place in his empire the money could have been coming from.

Perhaps it was the chance to scope out the strip clubs, perhaps he wanted to make it up to Larry. Either way, Jordan was more than willing to follow the trail of contributions.

The next video was dark and grainy, but you could still see women in various stages of undress gyrating on a small platform around a pole. Strategic parts of their bodies were blurred by the TV censor. A dancer reached out a tattooed arm to a member of the audience and pulled back a bill with a sexy smile. No wonder they waited until ten o'clock to show this.

A man in a suit in the foreground watched, grinning.

"That's Max Rossi, folks. News One has discovered that Rossi owns or holds interests in several strip clubs on the South Shore of Staten Island, including The Rendezvous, The G-String, and Stilettos, where a recent drug bust nabbed the kingpin of the DeCicco circle, the notorious prescription drug ring that the mayor pledged to take down."

A photo montage of exterior shots of other even shadier-looking places swept across the screen. Larry didn't recognize any of them. He didn't know if this was a testament to his impeccable character or a disappointing reflection of his status as a hot-blooded male.

"Now, strip clubs are legal in the state of New York, though they have been less than welcome in this borough. Any betting was run through a sports book based in New Jersey, where gambling is legal. And Rossi has not been connected in any way to the drug bust." Jordan paused for drama. "But I asked the executive directors of the Secret Wish and Genie's Lamp Foundations how they feel about Rossi's connection to these business enterprises."

The image cut to an uncomfortable-looking Secret Wish

Foundation executive behind a desk, lips pursed. "Had we known where the money was coming from, we might have done without the new playground for the children," she said.

Another foundation executive came on screen, this time from the Genie's Lamp Foundation, a man whose necktie looked like it was about to strangle him. "We did think it was odd that the cash donation we received was in small bills," he said with a strained laugh, "but it was delivered by Mrs. Rossi herself, so we didn't think twice."

Larry choked on a sip of water. It made him hate Max even more to think that he would involve his wife and the mother of his child in his shady dealings. Monica deserved better. He would give her a much better life. He could make her happy.

When they'd kissed that day in the car, it was as if the simmering pot of water within him started to boil over. If Monica still wanted to be with her husband, if she told him that Max was the man for her, he would respect those boundaries, detestable as they were, and he would sever ties with her. But she didn't. She hadn't. And now her husband was in the news for all the wrong reasons.

It was just a matter of time.

Chapter 28

Larry went to a local florist and bought a small bouquet of peonies. He could have gone with roses, but they were too easy a choice, a romantic default. He wanted something different. He tried to push the thought out of his head that he had never once bought flowers for Sarah. It wasn't a decision made from coldness or an unwillingness to part with good money over something that would shrivel up and die in a few days. Rather, flowers were something she bought for herself and arranged in their living space to her own liking. As an interior designer, she knew far more about floral arrangements than the average person. Just as she had given up on making coffee or toast for him, he never attempted to buy any flowers for her. Still, was that an even trade?

With the bouquet in the passenger seat, he got breakfast at the drive-through window, then drove to the gym, where he waited in the back of the parking lot for Monica's morning cycling class to finish. He'd polished off his coffee and breakfast sandwich before she emerged.

He got out of the car and brushed the crumbs of his bacon and egg on a croissant off his lap. He waved at her as she came out the front door. She broke out into a run toward him.

In the romantic comedy in his mind, he would have run to meet her in a wild embrace. But he was still full from breakfast and didn't want to get indigestion. Plus, she was much faster and in better shape than he was. He decided to wait for her in the car instead.

She flung open the passenger door.

He gazed up at her beautiful face.

Her beautiful, furious face.

He swallowed hard, tasting for a second time the breakfast sandwich.

He offered her the flowers.

She sniffed the peonies, then used them to smack him in the face. Petals exploded all over the interior of his car. Peonies were a bad choice. Roses would have held up better.

She got into the passenger seat and slammed the door. "What the actual fuck? How could you do this to us?"

For a fleeting moment, he thought she was talking about himself and Monica, but then saw his mistake. "Um, wasn't it Max who—"

"Don't pull that high and mighty bullshit with me. You unleashed that idiot Jordan on us."

This was not going well.

"Let me see if I have this straight. You help him organize this whole media circus, hoping that when I saw what a miserable sack of shit my husband is compared to how *wonderful* you are, we go galloping off into the sunset?" She sang the word "wonderful" for emphasis.

He tried not to wince, but she was out of tune and the effect was painful.

"Spoiler alert: I know what a miserable sack of shit my husband is!"

"Let me—"

"It is *not* your turn." Her eyes were hot. But her face was frozen. She must have had the fillers done again. "Did you think I was that dumb? I knew what was going on."

"Sorry, what?"

"You saw the news. You heard what the executive director said. I delivered the donation. I counted the cash myself. You think I didn't know where the money was coming from?"

He stared out at the senior citizens as they showed up for nine o'clock water aerobics, carrying pool noodles just like the little kids. One old gal yelled out, "Marco!" to which the other silver-haired ladies answered, "Polo!"

"My husband is many things. But he is not inconspicuous. Do you know how many times I've walked into his office and caught him talking to one of his girlfriends on *speakerphone*?"

He stared down at the crushed petals all over the seats and floor. He would need to grab a bunch of quarters and head over to the gas station at the Bay Street Mini Mart to vacuum this mess out. The sweet scent sickened him.

"The money part was my fault. Our deal was that if he insisted on investing in those kinds of places, because God knows he was their best patron, he would have to give most of his profits to charity. And because men are assholes and they visit these places, there are so many profits! Believe me, there were many sleepless nights when I tried to ignore the fact that those women at The Rendezvous were responsible for renovating the children's wing at the hospital."

His hand twitched. He put it on the dashboard to steady it.

"And here you are. Thinking you're Prince Charming here to save Sleeping Beauty. No, not her. *Rapunzel*. You think I'm locked away in some tower? You're damn right I am. But I don't need rescuing."

A shriveled-looking man wearing a bathrobe, a Speedo, and swim goggles ambled by in flip-flops. The things old people can get away with. Rich people were supposed to get away with things, too. When would that superpower kick in for him?

"You like your life." He meant it as a question, but it came out as a statement.

"People stop what they are doing when I walk into a room. They look at me. They talk to me. They talk about me. Sure, not all of it's good. Gossip is inevitable. But what's important is that I'm the topic of conversation. I'm the one in the photos." She sniffed, then she started to scrape up the bruised petals.

"And you." She looked at him. "You want to fade into oblivion. All that money. Nothing to show for it." She dumped the petals into his half empty coffee cup.

"I was still drinking that."

"I know what I sound like. I'm all about myself. You're mostly right." She began to tear up again. "But I love him so much."

"You mean—"

"My son, you idiot. I love my son. I'm so afraid of what this news will do to him."

As if on cue, Sammy bounded out of the gym. Larry's stomach lurched. He hadn't considered her adorable little boy in any of this.

"You kept him out of school today?"

"No school. Teacher convention." She reached into her gym bag for a tissue and dabbed at her eyes. She blew her nose. It sounded like one of the Canada geese that liked to crap all over the big lawn at the condo complex. The homeowner's association had scheduled a meeting that night to discuss humane ways to keep the geese off the lawn. On the way down in the elevator this morning, a neighbor asked if he would be going. He'd said no. He'd assumed he'd be somewhere (not the diner) having an intimate dinner with Monica.

She gave her nose another blow and opened the door and got out with a quick wave. Hand in hand, they walked to her car.

Whether that was a "goodbye for now" or "goodbye for good" wave, he didn't know. But he was certain any plans he had hoped to have that evening with Monica were dashed.

Maybe he would end up going to the meeting about the stupid geese after all.

Chapter 29

The press conference was set for 9:30 on the morning of April 21, Natasha's eighteenth birthday. Because of all the hoopla surrounding Larry's win, plus the added drama of signing over the Made in the Shade winnings to Natasha, the New York State Gaming Commission deferred to him and his attorney as to where the press conference would be held. His attorney suggested that they have it at his law office. Larry, ever more accustomed to his eccentric rich man role, agreed that keeping the press conference closer to home would be convenient. Still, he asked if they could have it outside the actual office building, in the parking lot.

"You know, for a speedier exit." He imagined himself pulling a *Dukes of Hazzard*-style getaway by sliding over the hood of a waiting car after the last camera flash popped. He'd hop into the passenger seat and be driven off by whomever to wherever. He still needed to work out those details, but seeing as it was a big parking lot, he figured it could work out well.

The attorney had raised an eyebrow but didn't object. He no

doubt saw it as free advertising if they kept his firm's logo on the front awning in view of the cameras.

Larry dressed in a pair of black slacks and a gray button-down shirt. He considered wearing a tie, but after wearing the lanyard around his neck for all those weeks, his neck was rubbed raw. His time at the gym was paying off, and his clothes were starting to hang on him. He would have liked to dress better for the occasion, but he hadn't felt like going to any stores. There was always online shopping, but he was afraid that Sarah might intercept the packages for her cause of the week. He would have to tighten his belt for now. Then he remembered the guy who dressed as Batman at the press conference to announce his lottery win. He concluded his attire was just fine.

It had poured overnight, but the sun was peeking out from behind the clouds by the time he met his attorney and James, Gaurav's friend from the Gaming Commission, to go over a few final things before the press conference. In the end, he drove his own SUV. There was no way he was vaulting himself over the hood of that, getaway driver or not, so he parked in the very last spot of the parking lot, far away from the podium set up right under the office's awning.

At 9:27 a.m., he took his place in front of the members of the media. All the local TV affiliates were there, as were reporters from the *Advance*, the *Daily News*, and the *Post*. Having never been at a press conference before, he was surprised to see how many people were needed to operate cameras and microphones. Jordan, looking very much in his element, saluted him before he headed over to the News One camera to record a brief intro.

Aside from John, Natasha, and her mom, who looked like a slightly older version of her, there was no one except for a few clients at the nail salon next door, who glanced over at the group before heading inside for their appointments. Out of courtesy, he had told Sarah when the press conference was, but he anticipated her being deep in the trenches of whatever community project she had chosen next. In a moment of weakness, he had also texted Monica, though he knew full well that he should have saved his thumbs the energy.

At 9:35 a.m., when it was clear that no one else besides the actual press was going to show, Larry and his attorney were given a thirty-second warning. They stood to the right of the podium. James stood behind the podium and tapped the microphone three times to test it. It thunked in reply. "Good morning." His voice was clear and practiced, but he was too loud for the size of the crowd. He dialed back the volume, his expression one of disappointment.

The microphone check had been loud enough to capture the attention of the women in the nail salon. The door swung open, and out came several nail technicians and clients. The nail techs gripped the arms of their clients, who took careful steps in their flip-flops so they didn't smudge their wet toenails. A woman with her long nails polished in a shade of pink bright enough for Larry to see from where he was brought up the rear. She wore regular shoes and stood off to the side, gliding her hands through the air to dry her nails.

His stomach was a cauldron of bubbling anxiety with a healthy dash of what-the-fuck-am-I-doing-right-now? thrown in for added flavor. Here he was, Larry Sortino, about to become wealthy beyond imagination and have it documented on live television for all to see.

He didn't comprehend a word of what James or his attorney said to him. It was as if everyone were speaking a different language. He smiled and nodded, which appeared to be enough.

Natasha was called up to the podium. The card was handed over. James made a big show of giving the check to Larry, then ripping it up and giving a new check to Natasha. Everyone laughed. John hooted and jumped around like he was courtside at a Knicks game. Her mother let out a scream and applauded. One of the cameras panned over to him to get a shot. Happy people made for good television.

Larry was grateful that Natasha could share all this attention with him. She hugged him again, and he tugged one of her braids. Her parents invited him to her high school graduation party that June. He knew he'd be invited to her college graduation, perhaps her wedding, too. As a reward for giving her the prize, she had given him a place in her life. It felt genuine and not mercenary. He hoped he was right.

The cameras turned to Natasha, and her parents came up to the podium to join her. For a moment, Larry was out of the spotlight. What would happen if he ran away now? Everyone already knew his identity. Wasn't that enough for the Gaming Commission? Couldn't his lawyer accept the check on his behalf? He would double, triple his retainer for the inconvenience.

He watched a car drive into the lot and park. The driver got out and walked toward the crowd.

Monica. She'd come after all.

He took a deep breath and stood up straighter. His stomach lurched. He tried to focus on what the lottery representative was saying, something witty that made the reporters laugh. His attorney patted him on the back and smiled. He heard words, sounds, laughter, but none of it made sense. He needed subtitles to translate his own life.

This was what he understood so far—he was alone and had more money than he could spend in three lifetimes. It wasn't right. He would end up one of those sad sack lottery stories after all. He never wanted to become a story, sad or otherwise. He just wanted to live his life. When did that become such a tall order?

He heard his name. His lawyer nudged him. James reached out his hand and smiled. They had come up with the idea to do something dramatic for the cameras—Larry would hand him the ticket and get the numbers validated live on television.

He pulled the ticket from one pocket. Everyone cheered.

Then from the other pocket, he pulled a cigarette lighter.

What came next involved no flourish, no grand gesture. This wasn't a magic show, although later, a few of the onlookers from the nail salon would likely wonder if what they saw was real.

He flicked the lighter and touched its flame to the ticket that he had worn around his neck for nearly three months. It ignited.

He had practiced at home over the kitchen sink with a losing ticket someone had torn in half and left behind on the counter at the Bay Street Mini Mart. The practice ticket had caught fire easily and burned low and slow. The paper had curled into a loose cylinder and turned black. He had dropped it into the sink to extinguish the flame. The charred remains had shown no intelligible numbers. Perfect.

He should have known that he couldn't mimic the conditions in the outdoors. He also hadn't counted on the wind as it swept through the open parking lot. It was enough to fan the blue flame into a small, hand-held conflagration.

An audible gasp from the crowd. The woman with the pink fingernails began to flutter her hands in distress, then claw at the air around her as if she were struggling to stay upright. The other ladies with their half-finished pedicures started to shift from one foot to the other until their nail technicians tapped their arms, reminding them not to smudge their toes.

Natasha waved to the camera as her parents dragged her to their car. They all got in and sped away, no doubt grateful that Larry did not try out his latent arsonist tendencies on the Made in the Shade card.

He was lulled by the flame until he dropped the ticket to the asphalt with a yelp. The crowd gasped. It sounded like they were gearing up for a group attempt to blow out the flame. The ticket missed a puddle, but instead, it caught the corner of a small spot of engine oil. The ticket flared brighter, a miniature bonfire. He stared into the flames and forgot where he was for a moment.

A muffled cry rose from the back of the astonished crowd. He turned away from the small inferno to see who was causing the commotion.

Stunned, he watched as Monica catapulted herself out of her sky-high heels and dashed barefoot across the asphalt to the front of the crowd. She grabbed a water bottle out of one of the reporters' hands and dumped it on the flames. But she was too late. All that remained was the black ash of the lottery ticket, exactly like the practice ticket in the sink. He sighed with relief. Something had finally gone according to plan.

She sobbed with a level of emotion that he had only ever seen on a news report that showed the aftermath of a cave collapse somewhere on the other side of the world. He had watched as a group of men carried the limp body of one of the dead and a trio of women walked alongside, an impromptu funeral procession, wailing and waving their arms heavenward. Their reactions were understandable. Their loved one was dead. But Monica's behavior was repulsive. He stared at her in disgust as she carried a sliver of the charred ticket in her hand like an injured animal. He groaned, his toes curling in his shoes as he watched her step right into a mud puddle. She didn't seem to care.

It wasn't about him. It was never about him. It was always about her. And money.

He walked over to her. She turned her big blue eyes to him. He had nothing more to say to her except, "Goodbye, Monica. Don't forget your shoes." He bent down to pick them up for her, but she swooped in to grab them, cradling one in each hand. Once her wails had subsided into shaky sobs, she nodded, then turned back toward the ash pile.

Saying goodbye again should have been agony. But the second time was much easier, even though the word "goodbye" was strange. His signoffs had always been less formal. "Later" or "So long" were much more his style. Casual dismissals that ensured the leave-taking was temporary. But this was goodbye. "Goodbye" was more permanent, had more sticking power. He was okay with that because it didn't hurt at all. He felt nothing.

When he fell in love with Sarah, there had been no angst, no misunderstanding. It was easy. Nothing but joy, albeit amid the ashes of September 11. When he allowed himself to see the truth, nothing had been easy in his relationship with Monica.

Not then and not now. None of it felt good. Did it ever? No. Not when they had been together that first time in college, and not when he had her in his arms again. It had never been right. The real Monica was a disappointment. He felt his face flush. It was embarrassing that it took him this long to comprehend it.

Monica kneeled and bent over the charred remains of the ticket, her version of the Pietà. She turned to him, the ashy bits of paper in her trembling hands. Her eyes begged him to fix it, fix this, fix her.

But he couldn't fix her. She didn't want to be fixed. She would go back to her big house on the hill with Max and little Sammy, and she would slip right back into the routine of her life. She got up and stumbled to her car, carrying what was left of the ticket in one hand, her shoes in the other.

He would never see her again in person. Of course, her picture would continue to be in the local newspapers alongside Max. The tide of popular opinion had turned back his way once more. Just two days after the newscast, he came to the rescue of a patron choking on a mozzarella ball in his hotel's restaurant.

Larry shook his head hard. He wouldn't linger over those photos anymore. He would erase Monica from his mind. And this time, he was happy to see her go.

Without even bothering to get a comment from him, all but one of the reporters were rattling off their take on this unusual turn of events. They told the viewers at home there was nothing wrong with their televisions or their streaming devices, that it was indeed just a very odd Staten Islander renouncing his fortune in an actual blaze of glory.

Larry walked back to the podium. He flipped the switch to the off position on the microphone. No one needed to hear any more from him, and that suited him just fine.

He shook hands with his lawyer and bumped fists with James. "Much appreciated, gentlemen."

"I'll send a bill," said his lawyer.

"Anything for a friend of Gaurav's," said James.

The one reporter not babbling into a microphone was Jordan. There he was with that incorrigible smile, shaking his head at Larry. Perhaps when the dust settled, he would call Jordan and they would meet up somewhere for a drink or a bite to eat. Maybe not. He thought he deserved better friends at this point in his life. But he wouldn't worry about that now, and he wouldn't worry about Jordan. His tuition payment for Jordan's one-year intensive broadcast journalism program at New York Film Academy ensured that he was safe from any other future scoops.

Larry tipped an imaginary hat to his former colleague. His work here was done.

He began walking to his car but stopped. A lone figure stood beside it. He smiled.

It was Sarah. When he saw her, he remembered everything that was good and nothing that was bad.

She walked toward him, and he walked faster toward her. His heart drummed in his chest. Here she was. His love. His partner. She was the one.

She smiled even wider as he approached, so happy to see him. The exact opposite, he supposed, of how most soon-to-be ex-wives were when they ran into their soon-to-be ex-husbands.

She reached out to touch him, then drew her hands back and put them in her coat pockets. "Lah, what have you done?" She gave him that familiar smirk, the one that reminded him so much of the old Sarah that he struggled to breathe.

She had been in the back of that absurd crowd the entire time, the single authentic figure at this whole spectacle. The one who had come to support him, the man, not his money. She was the only one he cared about.

"Have you lost all your common sense?"

Oh, that smile.

"Nah, there's still a bit around here somewhere."

She giggled.

And in that moment, he was certain they could be fixed.

He reached for her hands and slid them out of her coat pockets. She fell into him, her cheek against his chest. For a moment, he held her as she sobbed, as she had on their first night together, that terrible, tragic night.

"Remember what your mom used to say?" she said, her voice muffled by his coat.

He took a step back to look at her. "You'll need to be more specific. She talked a lot."

They both laughed.

He missed his mother. What would she have said about all of this? "What in God's name are you going to do with all of that money?" or something like that. All Diane Sortino ever wanted for her son was to be happy and safe. It's the reason she'd lied about his dad for so many years. He understood that now.

"She would say, 'Numbers don't lie. People do.'" Tears tumbled down her cheeks. "I'm so sorry, hon. I never wanted to prove her point." She squeezed her eyes shut. "I'm sorry for hurting you. For hurting us."

They faced each other, hand in hand. He recalled their wedding day when he stood with her at the altar. All he'd wanted to do during that endless hour in the church was take her in his arms right then and there, push past all that billowy white satin. They had vowed to love each other forever. They were getting that chance again.

He leaned down and kissed her. *This* was how it was done. This was how you showed someone there was no one else you'd rather be with in this moment in time, or any moment in time, for that matter. How lucky he was to have a second chance at a first kiss with the true love of his life.

He brushed a tear from her cheek. He took a deep breath in and let it out.

"Lah?"

"Mm hmm?" This breathing easy thing was wonderful.

"That wasn't the real ticket, right?"

"Sure was."

"That was a brave thing you did."

"Not really. I validated it about an hour before the press conference."

"Oh, thank goodness."

Her laughter was like music. He hoped it would be the soundtrack to the rest of their life together.

Acknowledgments

Larry and Co. have been floating around in my brain for more years than I care to admit. I owe a debt of gratitude to the following people, who encouraged me to finally introduce this wacky cast of characters to the world:

Mandy Miller, my talented editor at Literary Wanderlust, who knew when to coddle me and when to kick me in the butt.

Annalisa Parent and the Writing Gym community, who believed in me and my writing even when I did not. This novel would not exist without you.

Christopher Keane and Kevin Miller, my wonderful Emerson professors who supported me during very early drafts of Larry's story.

Rachel Eve Moulton, who proved so eloquently that if an idea for a novel sticks with you, you should stick with it.

Patricia Barletta, for her guidance and friendship.

Jean O'Toole, for her fierce wisdom.

George Esposito, Jr., for his level-headed insight.

Erica Carboy and Kristen Krista, charter members of the Larry Sortino Fan Club.

Linda Bellesi, my incredible mother and my biggest fan.

Andrew Zito, my favorite person and my muse.

And lastly, to the late, great Russell Bellesi, whom I like to think is playing his weekly lottery numbers at some convenience store in the sky.

About the Author

Barbara Bellesi Zito is a freelance writer covering real estate and home improvement trends for various media outlets. She earned her BA from Wagner College and her MFA from Emerson College. Barbara lives in Staten Island, NY with her husband and their dog. *Lucky Stiff* is her first novel.

Follow Barbara on Twitter, Instagram, and Facebook: @BarbTheWriter

www.barbthewriter.com

CPSIA information can be obtained
at www.ICGtesting.com
Printed in the USA
LVHW030135211222
735553LV00006B/196